"I need to know who that man was and why he was here."

"I wish I could tell you." Rachel walked away and stared at the brightly lit Christmas tree, which was waiting for Saturday afternoon decorating to commence. "I was outside waiting for permission to talk to you. I saw the man slip through your gate. I can't say with certainty that it's because of my investigation. Nothing would indicate you're in danger. It very well could have been a home invasion gone wrong. Other than the Christmas tree, your lights were off. Your TV was on. Your car is in the garage. Maybe he thought the house was empty, that those two devices were a bluff. Christmas is prime time for thieves and porch pirates."

Maybe. Except the house wasn't empty. And Marshall didn't keep his gun handy, because he never wanted to risk Emma finding it. So if an armed man had kicked in his back door...

He and his daughter might both be dead.

Jodie Bailey writes novels about freedom and the heroes who fight for it. Her novel *Crossfire* won a 2015 RT Reviewers' Choice Best Book Award. She is convinced a camping trip to the beach with her family, a good cup of coffee and a great book can cure all ills. Jodie lives in North Carolina with her husband, her daughter and two dogs.

Books by Jodie Bailey

Love Inspired Suspense

Freefall
Crossfire
Smokescreen
Compromised Identity
Breach of Trust
Dead Run
Calculated Vendetta
Fatal Response
Mistaken Twin
Hidden Twin
Canyon Standoff
"Missing in the Wilderness"
Fatal Identity
Under Surveillance
Captured at Christmas

Alaska K-9 Unit

Deadly Cargo

Visit the Author Profile page at LoveInspired.com for more titles.

CAPTURED AT CHRISTMAS

JODIE BAILEY

LOVE INSPIRED SUSPENSE
INSPIRATIONAL ROMANCE

LOVE INSPIRED® SUSPENSE
INSPIRATIONAL ROMANCE

Recycling programs
for this product may
not exist in your area.

ISBN-13: 978-1-335-72279-9

Captured at Christmas

Copyright © 2021 by Jodie Bailey

This edition published by arrangement with Harlequin Books S.A.

For questions and comments about the quality of this book, please contact us
at CustomerService@Harlequin.com.

Love Inspired
22 Adelaide St. West, 40th Floor
Toronto, Ontario M5H 4E3, Canada
www.LoveInspired.com

Printed in U.S.A.

The thief cometh not, but for to steal, and to kill, and to destroy: I am come that they might have life, and that they might have it more abundantly.
—*John* 10:10

To Jessica Patch

You challenge me to think bigger, to think deeper, and to take these stories beyond where they would ever go without you on the other side of my text messages.

And, you know, because the only way to rescue someone from a wood chipper is to use a Star-Lord.

ONE

The small residential street was quiet, dusted with a brief afternoon snowfall. The dozen houses along both sides of the narrow road were decked out in Christmas tree lights and sparkly decorations. If she wasn't undercover trying to catch a spy, the scene would be idyllic.

"We've been looking at this all wrong. We're back to square one, without a single suspect. It's past time to read the captain in on our investigation." Army captain Rachel Blake adjusted her earpiece and shifted to a more comfortable position in the front seat of her rented blue sedan.

From his desk at Eagle Overwatch headquarters several hundred miles away in the North Carolina mountains, Major Gavin Harrison didn't immediately answer. Only the creak of his chair said the line was still open.

"Sir, I've been at Fort Campbell operating as *Lieutenant Shelby* in this company for three months." She emphasized the undercover name they'd set up for her when the operation began. "In those three months, my team has uncovered four more hard drives for sale on the dark web. Four more hard drives that tie back to this infantry unit. Somebody, somehow, is getting their hands on those drives. We've cleared the captain of this company because he wasn't within eight thousand miles of the first theft, and we need him involved. He has knowledge we don't."

Plus, she needed more eyes than her own. Calling in her team now would be risky. This was a solo undercover mission for a reason. "I need your permission to talk to Captain Slater."

"I'll run it up the chain of command as soon as we hang up." Major Harrison exhaled loudly. "The potential breaches in intelligence if those hard drives fall into the wrong hands are huge."

Dragging her palms down her cheeks, Rachel wished again for coffee. She already knew everything he was saying. It all rested on her shoulders.

"I'd like to talk to him tonight. It's—" She leaned closer to the windshield. Had she really seen that?

She had. A dark figure crept across the side yard toward Captain Marshall Slater's stone-and-siding two-story.

"Blake?"

"Somebody is breaching the captain's yard. I'll keep you posted." She killed the call, pulled the earpiece from her ear and tossed it onto the seat. Snatching a black ski mask, she pulled it over her head and crept out of the car, keeping to the shadows as she eased her way across Captain Slater's front yard to a position between the bushes and the house.

In the damp December darkness, footsteps around the corner crunched on the recently fallen dusting of snow.

Listening for more sounds from the backyard, Rachel pressed her back against the house. She pulled her SIG from its holster and gripped it with both hands, keeping the barrel aimed at the ground.

From behind the closed curtains at the front picture window, Christmas lights tinted the thin snow in the front yard with a pale, dancing sheen. The muted sounds of a classic holiday cartoon drifted from the room where father and daughter watched television, oblivious to her presence outside.

And unaware of the shadowed figure Rachel had watched disappear through the gate in the privacy fence.

Angling her head, she tried to pinpoint where the intruder might be lurking. It wouldn't be wise to open the gate without some idea of where the threat might be.

She hoped none of the neighbors would spot her dark-clothed, face-covered self hiding behind the bushes. Her cheek itched under the balaclava, but wearing it was necessary to maintain her cover.

Only the sounds of the TV broke the late-evening stillness. The eerie silence from behind the house set Rachel's teeth on edge. She'd seen someone slip into the yard. She had no doubt someone was back there.

But they weren't moving. There were no more snow-crunching footsteps.

Either they'd walked too far around the back of the house before she made it across the street from her car, or they knew she was out there and were waiting to see what she'd do.

A standoff between good and evil.

Her watch vibrated against her wrist, and she glanced at the tiny screen. Update.

With a quick tap, she sent back a fist emoji, her investigative unit's accepted shorthand for *Hold tight. Nothing's changed.*

Pulling her black jacket sleeve down to cover the watch face, she eyed her footprints in the yard. The snow forecast for tonight had better be heavy enough to cover her tracks. Otherwise, the Slaters might wake up to the stark knowledge that someone—make that two someones—had been skulking around their yard in the darkness.

She couldn't wait any longer. Whoever had made their way through the Slaters' gate was still back there, and there was no telling what they were doing or how much danger they were about to rain down on the small family.

There was no way of knowing why the person had targeted them, either. Was it about her undercover investigation? Or was it something else entirely?

Regardless, no one got to traumatize a father and daughter who'd already known too much pain.

Regulating her breaths, Rachel pushed away from the house and crept along close to the dark gray stone where the eaves had prevented the day's earlier light snowfall from hitting the ground. She rolled her feet from heel to toe as she walked, careful to remain silent. There would be no telltale crunching from her footfalls.

At the gate she stopped, held her breath, listened.

A slight scrape came from the wooden deck on the back of the house. Since no breeze stirred the trees, it had to be the person she'd observed.

No intel had indicated that Captain Slater was in danger, so what exactly was going on here?

There were too many unknowns, but a cloaked figure sneaking around his yard meant danger—maybe even death.

Rachel would not let that happen. She would not let his young daughter grow up an orphan.

Lifting the latch, Rachel eased open the gate and slipped through, weapon raised and steady in her hands. She slowly scanned the yard, which was lit only by soft light spilling from a rear window. No shadow moved.

Easing to the corner of the house, she peeked around to the deck.

A man dressed in black, his face hidden by an army-issued balaclava almost identical to her own, knelt by the back door, attempting to pick the lock.

One side of Rachel's lip lifted slightly. *Gotcha.*

If she did this right, she might be able to

take him down without Captain Slater or his daughter ever knowing they were in danger. She might be able to prevent that little girl from nightmares about faceless men roaming through her home.

Rachel shuddered, then dragged her attention out of the past and into the job at hand. She flattened against the house, tapped her watch with a pointing-finger emoji—*going in*—then raised her weapon and rounded the corner.

She was halfway to the deck when the man spotted her and rose, his hand moving toward his back.

"I wouldn't." Rachel kept her aim steady and her voice low as she lifted the hem of her black fleece jacket to reveal the badge at her hip. "Military investigator. Lace your fingers behind your head, walk slowly down the steps, turn your back to me and kneel." *And don't you dare make a sound that would scare that precious little kindergartner in the house watching TV with her daddy.*

The man hesitated, his gaze skittering to the side as though he were considering a jump from the high deck to make a run for it. He must have been smart enough to know he wouldn't get far because, with one last sneer at Rachel, he obeyed, his knees crunching softly in the snow as he knelt at the foot of the stairs.

SIG in one hand, she pulled her handcuffs from the hip pocket of her black cargo pants and approached her suspect. As soon as she had him cuffed, she'd pull that ski mask from his face. If this was about her investigation, she might find out exactly who the mastermind was behind a ring of thievery that had plagued the 101st Airborne Division for nearly a year. If it wasn't, she'd somehow managed to be in the right place to take a random thief into custody.

What were the odds?

"I know why I'm wearing a mask. Why are you, Officer?" The man kept his voice low, and he spoke with an atrocious fake Australian accent. The timbre of his voice was slightly familiar, but she couldn't place it. "You undercover?"

Her pulse quickened. He was too close to the truth. "Stop talking." The last thing she needed was for him to raise his voice enough to bring the captain outside.

Or, if he were from the battalion, for him to recognize her.

She lowered her arm to holster her weapon and reached for his right hand to cuff him.

He bucked as she reached for him, driving her to the ground on her lower back. Her pistol and handcuffs flew into oblivion. Her neck whipped, ripping pain down her spine. The jolt from her neck collided with the pain from impact in a blinding flash.

She tried to roll onto her side, but a damp, snowy boot caught her in the chest and pinned her to the ground.

When her vision cleared, the man stood over her, silhouetted against the light in the kitchen window. He was nothing but a gray shadow in her pain-blurred vision, but it was clear when he raised his hand that he held a gun.

It sounded like the Chavezes' cats had scaled the fence and tipped over his trash can. Again.

US Army captain Marshall Slater scrubbed the top of his head and glanced down at his daughter, Emma, who was curled up against his leg, fast asleep with a Winnie the Pooh doll tucked against her chest. One of her dark pigtails lay across her cheek. She'd conked out ten minutes into the Christmas cartoon she'd bubbled about all through dinner. Kiddo was exhausted from the excitement about her class Christmas party.

Leaning his head back against the couch,

Marshall stared at the ceiling, where the red, white and green lights from the tree created a pattern that blurred in front of his tired eyes. Maybe they could sleep right there on the couch. Maybe he could ignore the cats and deal with the garbage can in the morning.

Another crash made up his mind for him. If he waited until morning, those cats would have a week's worth of trash strewn from here to post. That would be no fun to clean up, especially if it snowed tonight on top of it.

He eased to the side and stood slowly, careful not to wake Emma, and padded across the hardwood, his socks slipping at the kitchen entry when another thud seemed to rattle the entire deck. What in the world were those cats doing?

At the back door, he slipped his feet into soccer slides, then flung open the door as fast as he could, hoping to scare the cats into quick motion across the fence into their own yard.

A curse blistered his ears, followed by another string of them in a thick accent.

The Chavezes' cats definitely didn't utter curse words.

Adrenaline surging, Marshall stepped onto the deck and turned toward the stairs.

Two men dressed in black, their faces covered, stared up at him. One was pinned to the ground by the other.

It was the one standing who stopped Marshall's heart. He held a semiautomatic pistol aimed squarely at the other man, and his calculating gaze shifted from Marshall to his victim.

As Marshall took another step onto the deck, the smaller man on the ground took advantage of his attacker's distraction and leaped to his feet. With a round kick worthy of any '80s action movie, he caught the other man's hand and sent the gun flying with a clatter against the side of the house.

The tall man stumbled, eyes wide with anger or shock. He moved as though he might attack again, but then he scrambled backward and made a run for the fence gate.

No way was he getting away to come back another day. Marshall bolted for the steps, determined to catch the retreating intruder, but his foot slipped on the snow-covered wood, and by the time he recovered his balance, the man had disappeared through the gate.

When Marshall made it to the fence, he was gone.

Tires squealed around the corner, and a

car's engine roared into the night. There was nothing he could do with the escapee, but there was one man to go.

Whirling toward the yard, Marshall scanned for the smaller of the two men.

Near the base of the stairs, the man struggled to get to his feet. The gun he'd kicked away from his partner lay only a few feet away.

Marshall scooped up the weapon and took aim before the man could rise. "Stop. Right there." He might not have both of his backyard intruders, but he could certainly hold this one at bay while he called the police. He pulled his cell phone from his sweatshirt pocket. "I don't know what your buddy and you were fighting about or why you were doing it in my yard, but the party's over." He pressed and held the volume and power button on his phone to activate an emergency call. *Connection in five, four, three—*

"That was most certainly not my buddy."

Wait. Marshall's fingers slacked on the phone, releasing the keys. That voice definitely was not masculine. It was either a kid or…

He gave the hooded figure a quick survey as it came to its feet, straightened and lifted its hands in surrender. That was definitely a female.

And that voice… He knew that voice. But from where?

"Who are you?" He steadied his aim but kept his finger flat beside the trigger rather than on it. "Were you with that guy?" He sounded like a babbling idiot, but his brain was still trying to comprehend the past minute and a half.

"I was trying to save you from that guy." The woman kept her hands raised, but she tipped her index finger toward her waist. "I'm a military investigator. I have a badge clipped to my belt on my left side. My ID is in the thigh pocket of my pants, if you'll let me show you."

Marshall jerked his chin up in assent, but he didn't lower the weapon.

Gingerly, she gripped the side of her jacket between two fingers and little by little lifted the hem.

A polished badge glinted in the faint light. Releasing her jacket, she raised her hand again. "I'm guessing you won't let me dive into my pocket for the ID."

Narrowing his eyes, Marshall continued to study her. She was trying to keep her voice low, but it was familiar. The tone tickled the back of his brain. Her stature, her build… He eased a few steps to the right, trying to see her eyes in the light.

They were pale blue.

With an exhalation that almost deflated his chest, he lowered the pistol. This night just kept getting weirder. "Lieutenant Shelby?"

Even beneath the balaclava, it was easy to tell from the motion of her eyes that she winced. She turned her head toward his deck and seemed to measure her words before she spoke. "Call the police. Tell them you had intruders in your backyard, but don't mention me. You need them to come and file a report and pick up that gun, although the only fingerprints on it are going to be yours." She stepped sideways toward the gate. "That makes it useless to me."

"Lieutenant." He put all the force of his command into his voice. If she thought she was simply going to walk out of this mess, even with a badge on, she was a lot less intelligent than he'd given her credit for the past few months.

She glanced toward the gate, then met his gaze again. Rather than look defiant, she almost appeared defeated.

"I'll call the cops once you show me your

ID, but you're not going anywhere. Seems to me you have a whole lot of explaining to do. And you're starting now."

TWO

Three country music artists had already put their signature twists on three Christmas classics, and Rachel was ready to shut off Captain Slater's TV. It wasn't the music. She actually enjoyed it on a regular day. Being this close to Nashville guaranteed she'd gained an affinity for the genre.

But if one more note poured out of the cordless surround-sound speakers, her head was going to explode. Even though the volume wasn't loud, the tunes seemed to echo between the vaulted ceiling and the hardwood floor. She sat on the edge of the couch and fought the urge to press her hands to her ears like an overstimulated kindergartner.

Kindergartner. Rachel cast a quick glance at the stairs that led to a railed balcony at the start of a hallway. The captain had called the police and, while they waited for officers to arrive, had gently lifted his sleeping daughter and disappeared up the stairs. When two patrolmen tapped on the door, he'd stepped onto the small, covered front porch with them to file his report. He'd been determined that his little girl would not have her sleep disturbed.

No thanks to Rachel, little Emma would wake up in the morning none the wiser to the danger that had crept up her home's back steps.

She should have called the police for backup instead of going it alone. She never should have let Captain Slater catch her.

Instead she'd rushed in and gone to battle to protect a soldier and his innocent daughter. Even though it would mean a definite chewing out from her commander come tomorrow, she'd likely do the same thing again if the need arose.

That might be her biggest problem. She kept repeating the same mistakes.

Well, that and her failure to protect the Slaters.

As a fourth country crooner, this one wearing a formfitting red dress, launched into yet another holiday tune, Rachel rocketed upward from the couch. She might have made mistakes tonight, but she wasn't going to sit around waiting to be called into the principal's office like a child. If Captain Slater wanted to talk to her, he had her phone number. Given that she still had to investigate, he would see her at work tomorrow. Sitting around watching a brunette bombshell with a twang simper about what she wanted for Christmas wasn't solving anything.

She'd made it two steps toward the kitchen and a back-door escape when a tiny voice drifted from above. "Where's Daddy?"

With an exhalation born of leftover adrenaline, Rachel froze, then turned on one heel toward the small figure who stood on the landing that looked down into the living room. Dressed in red flannel pajamas dotted with Christmas ornaments, Emma Slater was the perfect picture of childhood at Christmas.

But the crease in her forehead spoke of anything other than seasonal joy. No doubt she was suspicious of the strange woman in her living room.

Really, what had Rachel been thinking? Her cover was blown with the captain. She'd have to explain before she could bolt if she intended to keep investigating with his help.

Rachel stepped backward so that she could look up without craning her neck quite so far. Her heart went out to the little girl who'd already seen so much sadness in her short life, whether she remembered it or not. "He's out on the porch talking to some friends. He'll be in soon."

That seemed to satisfy Emma. She shoved braided brunette pigtails over her shoulders, then dropped to her knees and pressed her face between the white spindles. "I know you. You work with Daddy. You pushed me on the swing."

The girl had a sharp memory. They'd only met briefly at a battalion cookout in mid-October. "That's right."

"After the swings, I ate pumpkin pie. I remember that. It was good. I'd never had pumpkin pie before. But Daddy didn't let me put as much whipped cream on it as I wanted to."

Rachel grinned in spite of herself. "Well, your daddy was probably right. It's super easy to overdo the whipped cream."

"Especially when you're six." The masculine voice from behind spun Rachel on her heel, her earlier miss making her ready to fight now.

But it was Captain Marshall Slater who stepped into the house and shut the door behind him. He didn't look at Rachel but turned his attention to the top of the stairs.

Emma looked down at her father with wide eyes that said she knew she'd been caught and a teasing grin that said she also knew the consequences would likely be minor. "Hi, Daddy."

"Emma Kate, do you know what time it is?"

"Mmm..." She pressed her lips together and rolled her bright green eyes toward the ceiling, as though there might be an answer there. The air around her was tinged with little-girl mischief. "I don't know." She sing-songed the words.

"Yes, you do." The captain mimicked his daughter's musical tone. "It's bedtime. And if you want French toast for breakfast on Saturday morning, you'd better double-time it back under those covers."

Emma popped up like a jack-in-the-box. "G'night, Daddy. G'night, soldier lady who pushed me on the swing when I had pumpkin pie." She disappeared, and, somewhere down the hallway, a door clapped shut.

Captain Slater was still smiling when he lowered his chin and turned to Rachel. "Pumpkin pie?" He reached for the remote on an end table and put a merciful end to the twanging train of Christmas carols.

"That's where the whipped cream conversation started." Despite the gravity of their current situation, she flashed him a quick smile in return. It seemed they both needed a minute to step away from danger and breathe. "Apparently, the mandatory fun day we had back in October was the first time she ever had pumpkin pie, and you were stingy with the whipped cream."

His grin widened. "I'm such a mean daddy." Captain Slater walked past her and into the kitchen. "The way I remember it, Em liked the whipped cream more than the pie. She dug into a tub of the stuff with a spoon."

"That sounds about right for her age." Unsure of whether or not to follow him, Rachel stood in the center of the living room. With the front door clear, she could easily turn and leave. He really couldn't keep her here. He might or might not know it, but he wasn't actually in her chain of command. He was the commander of her fictional undercover persona's company.

It was possible he was already in the process of figuring that out, though.

The commander reappeared with two cans of citrus soda. He tipped one toward the couch, then handed it to her as he walked toward a leather recliner. "How do you know so much about kids Em's age?"

"I was a nanny in college. I helped out during the year and lived in full-time during the summer. The kids were two and four when I started, so I got to go through all the lower elementary years."

Cracking open his soda can, he took a long sip, then eyed her with wary interest. "So you were as driven in college as you are now?"

"You could say that." Rachel sat on the edge of the couch and settled her unopened soda on the low iron-and-glass coffee table. "Captain Slater, none of these questions are the ones you really want to ask."

"After what we've seen tonight, you can call me Marshall, at least in my own house. And you're right." He flicked at the top of his soda can, the tab clicking. "I'm actually taking a minute to process the past hour, and I'm also questioning my own judgment."

"How so?" This wasn't the path she'd expected their conversation to follow. It also wasn't the tone. She'd been braced for anger, disappointment... Definitely not chitchat or the regret she saw in his dark brown eyes.

"Well—" he scratched the day's stubble on his chin "—I found you in my yard fighting off an armed man. And then I left you alone in the house with my sleeping daughter."

"I would never hurt Emma."

"I would hope you wouldn't, but that was not my finest parental moment." His gaze never wavered. "I mean, sure, you showed me your ID, and I work with you, but what I've seen tonight—including the name on the identification you handed to me earlier—definitely does not match the Lieutenant Rachel Shelby I've been working with for the past three months."

Rachel bit the tip of her tongue. Until this moment, she wasn't certain if he'd actually read her ID and her badge. She'd hoped he had glanced at the photo and taken her word for it.

Even if he had, she'd still have to explain why she was at his house in a to-the-death wrestling match with an assailant. Still, she wasn't prepared to give away any more than she needed to. Not until she heard back from Major Harrison with permission from higher to spill the entire story. She'd texted him a brief summary of what had happened, and he was in the process of reaching out to their chain of command to get permission for her to tell Captain Slater the truth.

How could they deny her? She'd already laid out the argument for bringing him into the investigation, and they had no choice. After tonight's fiasco, continuing her investigation would be next to impossible without doing so.

She'd had a tough enough time convincing them he wasn't involved in the theft of the hard drives. The fact she was still alive tonight ought to solidify that they were right to believe her. If the man were guilty, he'd have already figured out why she was here and put an end to her. Right now, while she was alone with him in his house, would have been the perfect opportunity.

"So, Lieutenant…" Marshall rested the drink can on his knee. "I think it's time for you to tell me your story. Either that or it's time for me to call the police to come back and have you tell it to them." While his face was an unreadable mask, the tone of his voice was clear…

He was ready for answers. And Rachel's time on this investigation was running out.

Lieutenant Rachel Shelby held his gaze without wavering. She was good at whatever investigating she did—even better than she was in her job as a lieutenant in his company.

Check that. Lieutenant Rachel *Blake* was good at whatever investigating she did. That last name was all he'd seen on her ID, his attention too rocked by what he'd seen.

Marshall took another slow sip of his soda, letting the citrus fizz burn its way down his throat as he tried to figure out what to ask her next. Would she even answer if he could formulate a decent question? He'd threatened to call the police back to the house if necessary, but what good would that do if she really was who her identification said she was?

Tired of his waffling, she stood, her posture as straight as if she were at attention in a battalion formation. "It really would be best if you let me go now and we had this discussion some other time."

"Sit down, Lieutenant. Until I hear differently, you're still in my chain of command, so obey the order." He hated to use his command voice. Before tonight, he had never had to use it on her. She was buttoned-down and hardworking, meticulous to the smallest degree. One of the best lieutenants he'd ever worked with.

But maybe there was a reason she made certain to do her job well, to fly under the radar and try not to be noticed.

She eyed him as though his authority was under question—and it might be. But then she sat again, perched on the edge of his sectional sofa as though she could pop back up and leave at any second. "If I'm supposed to call you Marshall, maybe you should call me Rachel." Her voice was flat, but it held a force edged with winter chill.

"I have no idea what your real last name is, so that may be smart." If she was going to snap into hard-core mode, he would, too. He'd have to use his questions wisely, before her internal timer for this conversation ran out and left him with no answers. "Let's start with who the man in my backyard was."

"I don't know." The answer was quicker than he'd expected, firm and certain.

Marshall lifted one eyebrow. "You don't know? Or you can't tell me?"

"Believe me, my life would be a whole lot easier if I knew."

"Are you working with them?"

Her eyes widened, and her head drew back as though the idea had insulted her morals. "Absolutely not."

"So, you know why they were here."

"I don't."

This game of twenty questions was getting old fast. He was used to having his lieutenants obey without hesitation. Dragging answers out of one of them was outside his scope of experience. Especially given that she was sitting in his living room in civilian clothes.

All-black civilian clothes. "Let's cut to the

chase. Why were you in my yard, wearing a mask, doing your level best not to be seen?" *Wait.* She wasn't one of those women who stalked men of authority, was she? His stomach sank. The lieutenant he knew was better than that. At least, he hoped she was.

"Sir, you have to understand I'm caught in a situation that never should have happened. There's only so much—" She glanced at her watch, then pulled her phone out of the leg pocket on her cargo pants. With a quick nod as though someone on the other side of the screen could see her, she slid the phone back into place.

When she looked up at him again, her expression was different. Whatever that text said, it had shifted her into answer mode. "I've been cleared to read you in on my investigation."

Something about her tone made Marshall want to race up the stairs, pack up Emma and hide somewhere on the other side of the world. Whatever she had to say, it wasn't going to be good.

"That man outside? I truly have no idea who he was." Rachel finally opened her soda and took a long drink, as though she'd been dying of thirst and just waiting for permission to slake it. "Why am I here? Because

I've been here multiple nights, across the street, watching your house."

Had she really said that? Marshall sat up straight, prepared to lead her to the door and out of his life. "What exactly are you saying?"

Her gaze scanned from left to right and back again, as though she were reviewing a tape of the conversation in her head. Then her eyes widened. She held up both hands between them. "Oh! No. No, sir." Her cheeks pinked, and for an instant, he glimpsed what she was probably like as a young teenager.

She was clearly mortified. It was actually kind of cute.

Or it would be if the situation were any different.

"That was the wrong wording." She bit her lower lip, stared at the ceiling, then took a deep breath. Shoulders squared and maturity back in place, she looked at something just over his shoulder. "It's my job to keep an eye on you. Until today, you were suspected of passing intel from your company to the highest bidders on a dark-web site."

Marshall could practically feel the blood drain from his face. His heart worked double-time to get his system up to working speed again. "I was what?"

To her credit, Rachel said nothing. She simply waited for him to process.

There was a lot to process. Pressing his hands into the arms of his recliner, he pushed himself up and walked over to the fireplace. He braced his palms on the raw wood mantel and stared down at the dancing, gas-fed flames. The heat soaked through his blue jeans and warmed his legs from ankle to thigh. Somehow, it felt good to feel something outside himself that was as hot as the anger and confusion growing on the inside. It almost seemed to balance him. "You're with CID?" If intel was moving out of his company to bad actors in the world somewhere, then there was no doubt this had elevated to Criminal Investigation Command's level.

"No. I'm not."

He stepped away from the fireplace, his hands falling to his sides. Everything she said knocked one more ounce of energy from his already-sapped reserves. "Bigger?" There wasn't a lot bigger than CID. But what was bigger was the stuff of nightmares.

"I'm with Eagle Overwatch."

The words were simply and softly spoken, but they hit like a blow to the kidneys. He had to be dreaming, because there was no way this was his life. "Eagle Overwatch is real?" Every soldier in the army had heard rumors of a deeply buried investigative unit that operated outside CID's control. A unit that moved in when it was unclear how high up the issues went, or that stepped in when CID was overtaxed. Last year, a buddy of his at Fort Bragg had told him some crazy tale about an investigator who'd shown up to look into a contractor who was selling secrets, but Marshall had dismissed the story as urban legend.

"Overwatch is very real."

"Then shouldn't you be deeper in the shadows? *I can tell you what I know, but then I'll have to kill you* secret?"

She sniffed a small laugh. "Think of us like Delta or SEAL Team Six. Everybody knows we exist, but nobody is certain of what we actually do."

"But you've been investigating me." His name had crossed the desk of an agency so deep, he'd been convinced it wasn't real. There weren't many times in his life when his knees had weakened, but this was definitely one of them.

"You've been cleared." There was a soft sound, and then her footsteps drew near. She stood beside him, a couple of feet away, watching his profile. "We know it's not you, but all the evidence indicates that someone in your company is the guilty party. It seems to have started while your battalion was deployed, which is how we cleared you. You were here on rear detachment when the first drive was taken overseas. We're unsure if it's one person or if they've somehow managed to recruit multiple people. So far, we think we've intercepted every stolen hard drive, but eventually we'll miss one."

"If you haven't already." He dragged his hands down his face, stubble scratching against his palms. "There's a lot of data on those drives, from individual soldiers' personal information to classified intel. And I missed it moving out of my company. How much trouble am I in?"

"None, now that your name's been cleared, but…" She rested a firm hand on his shoulder. "I do need your help. You're the only one we've been able to fully eliminate as a suspect, which means everyone up to the battalion commander is out of the loop. I'm still the outsider. I didn't go to combat with this crew, so I'm not in the inner circle. You can see things I can't. You know who's acting differently, who's flashing cash they didn't have before, or worse, who's got a rebellious streak in them that could lead them down a seriously bad path."

"You know how this works, Lieutenant." He faced her and looked straight into her blue eyes. "Are you actually a lieutenant?"

"I'm Rachel when I'm in your house, remember? And I'm a captain."

He barked a sharp laugh. Just great. "So every time I've given you an order, including tonight…"

"I really didn't have to obey." She flashed a quick smile, one he'd often seen her use around the company. "Earlier tonight, I honestly was waiting for my chain of command to give me the green light to read you in. Otherwise, I'd have been gone before you came back into the house." Her gaze flitted to the side. "I'd probably have been gone anyway if Emma hadn't shown up."

"She's a great kid, but she's nosy like every kindergartner out there." He stepped away from the fireplace, glanced at the balcony and frowned. "I don't think she's listening, given that I threatened to take away her Saturday French toast, but you never know."

"I've been watching. No movement upstairs."

"Good." Emma tended to fight sleep like it was public enemy number one, but once she gave in, she was out for the night. A raging tornado couldn't drag her into wakefulness. Marshall ought to know. He'd hauled her snoozing form to the basement on more than one tornadic Tennessee night. It wasn't a chore. He'd throw his body in front of a bullet to protect that little girl.

Which was why he hadn't let himself think of the full implications of this night, why he'd focused on the investigator in front of him instead of the trouble outside his door. "I need to know who that man was and why he was here."

"I wish I could tell you." Rachel walked away and stared at the brightly lit Christmas tree, which was waiting for Saturday afternoon decorating to commence. "I was outside waiting for permission to talk to you. I saw the man slip through your gate. I can't say with certainty that it's because of my investigation. Nothing would indicate you're in danger. It very well could have been a home invasion gone wrong. Other than the Christmas tree, your lights were off. Your TV was on. Your car is in the garage. Maybe he thought the house was empty, that those two devices were a bluff. Christmas is prime time for thieves and porch pirates."

Maybe. Except the house wasn't empty.

And Marshall didn't keep his gun handy because he never wanted to risk Emma finding it. So if an armed man had kicked in his back door…

He and his daughter might both be dead.

THREE

Morning had come too soon.

Rachel propped her chin on her desk at the company and eyed the large analog clock above her door. It wasn't even lunchtime yet. The end of the duty day would never get here. With nearly all the soldiers in the company preparing to head out on leave for the holidays, the building bustled with last-minute activity, though none of it involved her. Inactivity equated to boring.

It also equated to antsy. While she'd been with the unit for nearly three months, she'd mostly been observing the soldiers and their routines. It seemed there was always someone around the building, and investigating deeper had proved to be difficult, although she'd managed a couple of forays into the S-6 shop for some quick searches. She'd narrowed her investigation to those serving in S-6 as the only logical place to be making the hard drive switches, because they were in charge of processing the old drives and sending them off to be recycled. But deep background checks on the soldiers who worked there had yielded no red flags. She could be wrong. Or she could be up against someone who was just that good at covering their tracks.

Christmas leave meant the place would soon be emptier than it had ever been. And with Marshall now involved, there was a lot more freedom to dig. She hoped she'd have this wrapped up by Christmas. If she could keep herself awake.

She'd stayed at the Slater home until past midnight, going over theories and reassuring Marshall that she would do everything in her power to protect him and his daughter.

Neither Rachel nor Marshall was convinced the break-in was targeted. No one in the battalion had given any indication that they knew an investigation was ongoing, and Marshall certainly hadn't done anything to tip anyone off. It had to be coincidence that someone had targeted the house for a break-in.

Although, Rachel didn't believe in coincidences.

She'd slept as late as she dared and had slipped back to Marshall's house, trailing his SUV from a distance as he dropped off Emma at school. No one else had followed them.

He would pick her up again around three o'clock, when school released. That might give them time to do some digging at the company this afternoon after everyone took off, but she needed to rest first, or she ran the risk of missing something.

Reaching for her now-cold coffee, she downed a bitter swig and logged on to her work laptop. She had noncommissioned officer evaluation reports to review. This might not be her real job, but she had to behave as though it were. The soldiers who were innocent under her command needed their careers to move forward, uninterrupted by their counterparts' illegal activities. That meant she had to play the part of lieutenant to the letter, which meant she was doing two full-time jobs.

No wonder she was ready to crash and burn.

When the words blurred on the screen and refused to project any actual meaning, she got up and grabbed her coffee mug, then headed for the common room, where the coffeepot was on as long as people were in the building. Soldiers thrived on coffee and energy drinks.

She nodded at Sergeant James Plyler, who sat in the same beat-up chair he'd been in all morning, updating Lieutenant Yancey's laptop. Although he worked in the battalion S-6 shop where her investigation was centered, his background threw up no red flags. She still watched him as closely as anyone else in the shop, though.

On the other side of the room, she greeted Sergeant Wylie Joseph, one of her team leaders, and Specialist Jeff Quincy. The pair were huddled around a laptop in the corner, reviewing what looked to be Quincy's goals for the quarter. Joseph took a special interest in the younger guys on his team, especially guys like Quincy, who'd had a few minor disciplinary issues lately. She'd have to note that on his eval.

She'd also have to note Quincy's negatives, not something she looked forward to.

Filling her mug from the freshly brewed pot, she cradled it in her hands and imagined the warmth ran up her arms and woke up her brain. Tapping her finger against the side of the mug, she listened to the men talk. Quincy was one she hadn't looked too deeply at yet. He'd been with the unit for a while and had been a stellar soldier overseas, but since they'd redeployed, he'd had several instances of being late to PT and being just a level below insubordinate. It was worth looking into.

"Good morning, Lieutenant."

The deep voice sent a delighted little run of goose bumps over her arms. Rachel turned slowly, dismissing whatever that feeling had been. She was tired. She was overworked. She was hopped up on caffeine. Any of those things could have made her react to the low timbre of Marshall's voice.

He leaned a shoulder against the metal door frame of his office with his arms crossed, watching her. A navy blue coffee mug with #1 Dad emblazoned in white dangled from his index finger. Captain Marshall Slater was one of those soldiers who looked like he was built to wear the uniform. "That's your fourth cup today, isn't it?"

"You're counting?" Had it really been that many? She ran through her morning intake and winced. "I think you're wrong, sir." It might actually be her fifth.

He arched one eyebrow. The deep lines around his mouth and the dark circles under his brown eyes told her he was running on his own caffeine-induced fumes. "I may have missed one of your trips, but it's been at least four." He pushed away from the door frame and walked toward her with his mug outstretched. "I can see the coffee maker from my desk. You and Staff Sergeant Ostendorf have both made multiple visits. I tend to notice things like that. Don't need anyone keeling over from a caffeine overdose on my watch."

Behind him, the other soldiers had stopped their various activities and were watching them. Specialist Quincy looked away when he caught her gaze, but Sergeant Joseph watched with interest.

Probably because it looked like Marshall was flirting with her.

She filled Marshall's mug, then slipped the pot back onto the burner. As she did, she gave him a nod, a silent *go ahead* to talk about what they'd discussed earlier. "I'm guessing this is not your first cup, either?"

"Three." He took a slow sip, then backed away to a more appropriate distance. "Someone tried to break into my house last night. Between the police and the worry, let's just say I didn't get much sleep."

"Really?" Rachel watched the soldiers behind him over his shoulder. They'd agreed to discuss the incident around the company to see if anyone reacted. "Are you and Emma okay?"

All three men now stared at them without looking away, interested but not sending any suspicious signals. Yet.

"We're fine."

Specialist Quincy leaned forward. "What happened, sir?"

Marshall walked over to the men. "It was a weird night. Let's just leave it at that." If they were handing out Academy Awards, he'd win best actor, hands down. Nothing in his words or his posture indicated he suspected anything of the men. "The police ramped up patrols in the area. It was probably an opportunist who thought the house was empty and was looking to steal our Christmas presents."

Rachel almost smiled. He'd provided enough info to get the scuttlebutt flowing. It wouldn't be five minutes before the entire battalion knew someone had tried to hit his house. There would be conjecture and outsize stories… And both Rachel and Marshall would be watching for reactions.

"Really?" Sergeant Plyler closed the laptop and stood. "Someone tried to break into your place?"

"Yes."

"Need backup?" Sergeant Joseph slouched

on the worn leather couch with his arm resting along the back. "Or have you got this?" Something about his tone implied he didn't think Marshall had *got this*.

Interesting.

Marshall ignored him. "Don't forget we have a battalion formation at 1130. Rumor has it they're cutting us all loose for the afternoon afterward. Holiday leave's starting early." He took another sip of his coffee and watched the men. "Speaking of that, the usual invite to Christmas dinner at my house stands. Just let me know before you leave today so I can get enough food." He looked over his shoulder. "Plyler, you still coming?"

"Wouldn't miss it, sir. I remember that turkey you fried at Thanksgiving."

"You ate Thanksgiving at the commander's house?" Sergeant Joseph sat up taller. "How'd I miss that invite? I was cramming down a fast-food burger on Thanksgiving."

"Beats me." Plyler shrugged. "He told pretty much the whole battalion they could come."

Quincy wrinkled his nose. "You'd let a guy like me eat dinner at your house with your family?"

"Why wouldn't I?" Marshall didn't take Quincy's bait.

Joseph wrinkled his nose, watching Marshall, who turned to him next. "You're welcome to Christmas dinner, Sergeant." Marshall tipped his coffee cup at all three men. "This time, I know you heard it."

"Quincy is right, you know. You have to be careful who you let around your family." Joseph eyed Marshall for a long moment. "And I don't know. I made some promises to my girlfriend."

"Girlfriend?" Specialist Quincy shoved his finger into the sergeant's bicep. "Seriously? Since when?"

Joseph shoved his hand away, but before he could respond, Marshall spoke. "You three go wrap up what you need to get done. Just see me if you're coming." He dismissed them and turned to Rachel. "Lieutenant, I need to see you about a couple of those noncommissioned officer evaluations you were reviewing."

"Yes, sir." This had nothing to do with an NCOER. He must have noticed something. She followed him into his office, smiling at an old photo of Marshall, his late wife and Emma that rested on a bookcase behind his desk. Despite the tragic end to Maggie's life, they looked like a laughing, happy family in the picture. She'd have liked to have had a life like that.

"Actually…" Marshall paused as he rounded his desk. He rapped his knuckles on the top of his laptop. "After formation, grab your computer and we'll eat lunch at the P/X food court. I could use a cheesesteak and a loaded order of fries."

"Yes, sir." But why lunch? Maybe to get away from the company? She turned on her heel and nodded to the men on the couch, deciding to forgo the coffee. She was jittery enough.

Still, she could feel their eyes on her as she walked away. It was hard not to turn around and see which one of them was watching. It hadn't been long since the army allowed women in the infantry, so the feeling wasn't unfamiliar as a woman in a man's world, but it never got easier. And today, any of the soldiers in the building could be one of the men she was trying to ferret out, which made them dangerous.

Marshall had added a touch of genius to his speech when he'd tacked on the news about an afternoon off. The word of his almost break-in would spread even faster. Rachel planned to be watching at that formation. Someone was going to look suspicious. With the CO openly talking about the crime, the guilty party might just show themselves if it was someone in the company.

Rachel wasn't certain if she wanted it to be or not. If it were a random break-in, the Slaters were safe. But if it were a soldier in the unit, then her investigation might draw to a close in time for her to truly go home for Christmas.

The trouble was, if it were someone close by, that meant Marshall and Emma Slater were in danger from an unseen enemy...and if Rachel didn't quickly find the bad guy, the Slaters could go down in the cross fire.

The lunch crowd at the base's P/X food court was thin, thanks to holiday leave and a short duty day for nearly everyone on post. The air was salted with the scents of burgers, cheesesteaks and fried chicken. For the first time since dinner the previous night, Marshall's stomach grumbled a complaint *for* food instead of against it.

Feeling hunger was a surprise. His gut had gnawed at him all day as he'd watched his soldiers go about wrapping up their work. They should be the people he trusted above all others, not the ones he had to suspect and wonder about. Suspicion had eaten away at him all morning. He had no idea how Rachel did this for a living.

Leaning back against the wall, he watched her order at the Japanese food counter. Even as she relayed her choices to the teenager at the register, her head was on a swivel, watching. It was the investigator in her.

It was also a trait he'd noticed almost from the moment she'd first walked into the battalion. She'd always been on guard, but he'd chalked it up to that hyperawareness of surroundings that dogged most soldiers when they came back from being overseas.

He'd dealt with it himself. Overseas, every piece of trash on a footpath might be a bomb, every pothole an IED. Walking through the mall with Emma after his last deployment, he'd noticed everything from the kid with the backpack to the guy with his hat pulled too low over his eyes. That day, they'd left before they even made it to the center court, his heart pounding with too many possible deadly scenarios.

He was thankful that the longer he was home, the less that hypervigilance affected him. But remnants still plagued his everyday life. He half smiled. If Maggie were still alive, she'd be thrilled to know he no longer managed to somehow nail every pothole on the road. She used to claim he had a radar that drew him straight to them. Marshall now avoided them with a wide berth.

Across the room, Rachel paid, then glanced around, looking for him. Unlike last night, when her dark hair had been pulled up in a high ponytail, she had it twisted low near her neck, per regulations when in uniform. She wore the uniform well, her posture straight with the authority she bore, even though she was several inches shorter than most of the men in her platoon, and definitely shorter than his own barely six feet.

When she turned, he gave her a small wave, and she headed his direction, not meeting his eye but watching the handful of other soldiers and families in the small eating area. Something in his chest expanded. Yeah, she was here with him. It somehow made him proud.

Although it definitely shouldn't, not considering their situation.

He had no idea why he'd asked her to lunch in the first place. They weren't discussing her investigation in public, and they could have easily knocked out the NCOER thing in five minutes in his office, but something had grabbed at him, something he couldn't define. And suddenly, he'd wanted more than a quick chat about evaluations before they rushed out the door and headed their separate ways.

He wanted to know who Captain Rachel Blake was. Sure, he knew her persona, Lieutenant Rachel Shelby, but after talking to her the previous night, he knew that wasn't her. Not exactly. Maybe the essence of her, but it wasn't her.

He wanted to know the real woman. The one who wasn't pretending to be someone else. The one who had spent her nights camped out in a dark blue sedan up the street from his house. The one who had faced down an assailant in his backyard and had come up fighting.

He scanned the gray ceiling and admitted the truth to himself. She intrigued him. For the first time since Maggie's death, a woman tugged at his attention. Rachel had since he'd been introduced to her, but he'd ignored the attraction, believing she was his subordinate.

This feeling could either be a good thing or a bad thing. Given that Rachel was here investigating his battalion, it probably was not a good thing.

Maybe they should both get their lunches to go.

But it was too late for that. She took a spot

leaning against the wall beside him. "Looks like everybody's clearing out for the holidays."

"Can't say I blame them. It's a big travel time, and everybody's ready to get moving. Based on the leave requests that passed across my desk, most of our people are planning to hit the road or the skies this afternoon or early tomorrow morning. The entire post will be a ghost town within twenty-four hours." He shifted slightly so her shoulder no longer brushed his arm and angled so that he could see her out of the corner of his eye. "I'm guessing you aren't taking any leave?"

She didn't look at him. "Not this year. You?"

Not this year. Because of the investigation. "I did, even though I'm staying in town. Time away is good, but I'll be available to help you look around."

They'd discussed him helping her do some deeper searches while everyone was away, but he knew her well enough to know she wouldn't let him take too much time away from Emma. Instead, Rachel would spend Christmas combing through evidence while everyone else was off celebrating with their families. Her work wouldn't take a holiday. She probably wouldn't even take time to eat a decent piece of turkey or exchange presents with anyone.

The thought of her alone on Christmas, prowling around the building instead of celebrating Christ's birth with people who cared about her, tugged at the family man inside him. Nobody should have to do that. Even soldiers on duty had something special planned for them on Christmas, even if it was only slightly elevated chow in the mess hall. "You should take some time to come by the house for lunch on Christmas Day. Or on Christmas Eve. Or both, given you'll probably be in the neighborhood anyway." It was a subtle way to say he'd noticed she had followed him to Em's school and to work this morning.

She lifted her chin and looked at him, mouth tilted upward with a sheepish amusement, though there was a serious glint behind her eyes. She took a deep breath and looked back out at the glassed-in room.

At the sub shop, a black-aproned counterperson called his name before Rachel could respond. Probably for the best. It kept him from having to hear her say no to his ludicrous idea. They were the equivalent of work friends, not hang-around-each-other friends. Then again, they weren't even coworkers, even though it looked to all the world like they were.

Which further complicated things. He gave the server a nod of thanks as he grabbed his tray. While, in truth, they were in different units and were the same rank, it looked as though he was a rank above her in the same unit. In appearance, it might look to anyone who misread the situation as if they were toeing a line the army didn't like toed, and that could open them up to a whole lot of scrutiny that her investigation definitely didn't need.

Not that he was planning on dating her. But it never needed to look that way.

He pointed to a four-seater in the corner and claimed it, setting his tray down and pulling his laptop out of his bag. If this were a working lunch, it needed to be a working lunch.

It wasn't long before Rachel joined him and opened her own laptop. She situated it to her right, then squared her food tray in front of her and unwrapped her plasticware. "I'll be fine over the holidays. I'm used to it."

It took him a second to drag his mind back into the original conversation. Regardless of what she said and what he'd just been thinking, now that she was across from him and her blue eyes were regarding him, common sense blew away on something entirely different. Something more emotional than rational. "I wasn't kidding." He unfolded a napkin and laid it on his lap. "We stay home for Christmas, and Emma's maternal grandfather usually spends most of the day with us. He lives a couple of hours away. And you heard me talking to the men today. It's a party." He reached for his sub, the juicy steak and melted cheese dripping off the sides. This was going to be a mess.

In more ways than one.

"Do you think it's wise this year to invite the soldiers? To your home?" She might be weakening. The way she poked at her rice instead of loading up a forkful spoke to a bit of indecision.

It probably wasn't, but he couldn't imagine not doing it. Sometimes, fear had to take a back seat to doing the right thing. "Maggie started this when she was alive. She never liked to see anyone alone on the holidays. She had a particular soft spot for the ones who had to pull duty on Christmas." He flashed a quick smile at the memory of Maggie packing up to-go boxes for him to run to the company while toddler Emma napped. That had been her last Christmas. On the surface, it had been a good one, not hinting at the dark shadows yet to come. "Last year, I had a few of the rear-detachment guys over while everyone else was deployed. Plyler and Jamison came to Thanksgiving. It's never a big crowd. Just one or two guys." As much as Marshall wanted the exchange to sound nonchalant, the words came out forced. He crammed a huge mouthful of steak, cheese and bread into his mouth. If he was chewing, he couldn't keep talking—not if he had half the manners his father had tried to instill in Marshall's rambunctious younger self.

Rachel stirred the rice again, added a packet of soy sauce, then finally took a bite. After she'd swallowed, she lifted her eyes to look at him, even though her chin stayed tilted downward. "Maybe. I'll let you know."

It took two tries to swallow the food he'd used to hush his own mouth. Chasing it with sweet tea finally restored his ability to speak back. "Emma's a trip on Christmas. I promise, it's not something you want to miss."

"I can only imagine." She smiled and seemed to shake out of whatever funk had gripped her earlier. "She's a cute kid."

"She is. I'm blessed to have her in my life." Marshall relaxed into the conversation. He knew from casual interactions around the battalion that Rachel was an open and friendly person with a sly sense of humor. And he had certainly noticed that she was almost regal in her uniform, with blue eyes that seemed to change with her mood. He'd heard the men in his company and knew not many of them had missed that, either. Learning that they were equal in rank and she was not in his chain of command had unlocked something inside him that noticed more than ever how beautifully unique she was.

Marshall reached for his sandwich again. "All the more reason you should hang out with us. You can't buy the kind of joy that kid brings to Christmas."

Something at the table changed. It was almost as though the air grew heavier, or maybe lifted away entirely, leaving a weight behind. Dropping her plastic fork, Rachel reached for her computer and shoved it in her backpack. She stood before Marshall could react and grabbed her tray. "I have to go. I'm sorry."

Marshall finally found himself and shoved his chair back from the table to stand, but she was already gone, striding away without an explanation.

FOUR

Please don't let him follow me. Please don't let him follow me.

Rachel shoved through the outside doors and leaned against the brick wall, gulping a chilled lungful of December air.

It wasn't enough. The gray clouds that had plagued the area and dribbled snow on them for several days felt close enough to touch and heavy enough to crush her. She tugged her beret on her head with shaking hands and pressed her back harder against the brick wall.

What had just happened in there? The last time she'd had a panic attack was more than two years earlier, shortly after she'd been called on the carpet for a slipup that nearly undid an investigation. Standing at the receiving end of her commander's stern glare, she'd been certain her career at Eagle

Overwatch was over only weeks after it had started.

What had triggered this rush of fear? She'd done nothing wrong. She'd been meticulous in tracking her work and in watching everyone in the company and around the battalion. Nothing about the conversation with Marshall had come even close to exposing the investigation to open air.

No, it was deeper than that. The image that had blindsided her at the table rushed in again and set up camp. The instant, unbidden portrait of a small family on Christmas morning, opening gifts in front of a roaring fireplace and a brightly lit Christmas tree.

The Slaters' fireplace and tree.

It was not a place she should ever envision herself. She was not part of their family. She wasn't a friend. She wasn't even a real coworker.

When she'd tried to have the dream, someone to love, it had exploded in her face. The pain and fear of that time hadn't hit her in years, not like it had today.

It couldn't hit her again. She was here to investigate, turn in her findings and move on once the bad guys were out of play.

She was not here to daydream about a family that could never be hers.

Rachel pressed her palms against her eyes. The issue was sleep. There wasn't nearly enough of it in her world at the moment. If she didn't hop off the stress treadmill soon, her emotions were likely to twist even more out of whack than they already were.

The sad fact of the matter was that she probably ought to call for backup, especially if it seemed the Slaters might be in personal danger.

But backup smelled of failure. Rachel couldn't risk a failure.

She dropped her head against the wall and managed three deep breaths that had her heart rate finally dropping back to acceptable levels. A nap was definitely in order because it wouldn't take much for her to fall asleep standing right here in her boots.

A shadow darkened the dim light from the snow-clouded sky. "Rachel?" It was his voice.

No surprise. Marshall Slater was the kind of guy with enough chivalry to come searching for the damsel in distress.

No way was she going to be the princess he needed to save. Taking an extra second to shove the image of him as a doting Christmas-morning father out of her head, she finally turned her head toward him. "Yes, sir?"

Why was she even trying to play this like she had no idea why he was standing in front of her?

"Are you okay?" He looked over his shoulder at the building's main entrance. "You ran out of there like I threatened to make you do a twenty-mile ruck march at dawn."

"I remembered I had to do something." Seriously? She really did need backup if that was the best she could come up with.

"Like hold up the P/X wall?" He rapped his knuckles against the brick. "Seems like a pretty stable structure to me. I don't think it needs your help." The words held amusement, letting her know he was teasing.

He was also digging.

Peeling herself off the wall, Rachel pulled her shoulders back and stood with her command posture. She might not be allowed to boss him around, but she could make herself look stronger than she actually felt. "It's not worth talking about right now. Or ever. I'm headed back to my apartment. Have a good afternoon, sir." She sidestepped and walked past him.

"You can stop with the *sir*." He fell in beside her. "I know what a panic attack looks like."

Rachel stopped, her boot hovering over the step-down at the curb.

"That definitely had all the hallmarks of one." He leaned closer. "What spooked you?"

Rachel shook her head, pulled every ounce of strength she had from her spine and faced him. They were practically nose to nose, and neither one of them backed off. It was a challenge. A standoff.

She was going to win.

"Nothing spooked me, sir. Now, you have a good afternoon." Snapping her head toward the front, she stepped off the curb and hiked her backpack onto her shoulder, striding away like she was entirely in command of herself.

She most certainly wasn't.

His footsteps dogged hers, but she didn't acknowledge him. She just wanted to get away. To go back to her rented apartment, curl up in the bed and sleep, preferably a dreamless sleep that didn't conjure a weakmoment family holiday fantasy about the man behind her.

He'd parked beside her in the middle of a row of cars, so she hoped he had accepted her *back off* message and was merely heading to his vehicle. That would be for the best. For a brief moment, she'd entertained the idea of friendship, but it was pointless. This had to stay professional, exactly like it would if he truly did outrank her in their chain of command.

Slipping between their cars, she clicked the remote to unlock the vehicle. Jerking open the door, she tossed her backpack across to the passenger seat, then moved to slip into her car, but something stopped her. Something was off. Wrong.

Rachel eased the car door shut and turned in a slow circle. Nothing seemed out of place in the parking lot. A handful of soldiers and their dependents walked back and forth between their cars and the building. No one seemed to be paying attention to her or to Marshall.

"What's wrong?" Marshall stood near the back of her car, between the sedan and his SUV. His posture was straight, his demeanor that of a man who was clearly on high alert.

She held up a finger and ran through her five senses. Often, something was tweaking at something that her brain hadn't quite registered yet. She saw nothing unusual. Heard nothing unusual.

Rachel pulled in a deep breath through her nose, but she stopped midinhalation. There it was. The hint of fish oil.

Except it wasn't fish oil. She'd learned that smell the hard way, after she'd investigated an accident that had taken the life of a young soldier at Fort Bliss.

Marshall stepped closer. "What?" He barely whispered the word.

"Brake fluid. And a lot of it." It was faint, but it was there, stronger near his SUV.

Taking a knee, Rachel leaned lower to look under his Ford Expedition.

And came face-to-face with a man.

As Rachel jerked backward, Marshall stepped away from her. Something was wrong.

As soon as Rachel recovered, she leveraged herself off the side of her vehicle and practically dived underneath his. "Go around. Stop him!" Her barked orders were muffled between asphalt and undercarriage.

Go around what? Stop who?

Rachel struggled with something beneath his Expedition.

Not *something*. She struggled with *someone*.

There was a grunt from under his SUV and a thud as Marshall sprinted around to the driver's side. A man leaped to his feet and sprinted away, the same dark ski mask the man in his yard had worn the night before pulled low over his face.

Marshall took off in pursuit. That man had tried to break into his house while his daughter lay sleeping. No way was he letting this guy slip through his fingers again.

The man dashed across an aisle as a horn honked and a silver minivan screeched to a stop, narrowly missing Marshall's fleeing assailant, who darted around the hood.

But the van rested in Marshall's path.

The driver stared wide-eyed and shocked as Marshall's feet stuttered to a stop.

He rounded the rear of the minivan as it eased away, but he stopped, heaving breaths of air as he scanned the parking lot. Where had the guy gone?

Other than the usual shoppers, no one appeared to be on the run or even paying attention to him.

He clenched his jaw and balled his fists. The guy could be anywhere. Behind a parked truck or in a getaway car. He could have shucked the ski mask and pulled off his jacket and blended in with the soldiers and families drifting in and out of the P/X.

Wherever he was, Marshall had lost him.

He shook out his hands, scrubbed his palm down his face and headed back to the vehicles. Ripping his phone from his leg pocket, he started to dial 911, then stopped. Rachel was on scene. It might blow her cover to call the authorities, and her team might want to do the investigating.

Wait. Rachel.

He'd left her behind.

Breaking into a jog, he reached his Expedition and her sedan to find her standing between them, facing his SUV with her phone to her ear and her other hand to her cheek.

When he walked up, she turned away from him and kept talking. "Thalia would be a good one. So would Fisher." Her voice sounded strange, strained and slightly off. "We're to the point of needing extra eyes." She listened for a second, nodding. "Sounds good. Out."

She punched the phone's screen and slid the device into her pocket, but she didn't turn. "He got away?"

"He did." Marshall stared at the back of her head. Her normally tightly wound bun hung half-unwound at her neck. She still held one hand to her face. "A minivan got between us, and he took off."

"The P/X has cameras. Our technical people will reach out through local authorities and get access to them."

Marshall narrowed his eyes and stepped closer, the gravel on the asphalt crunching beneath his feet. Her posture and her voice ran a chill along his arms. "You're not okay, are you?" He rested a hand on her shoulder.

She jerked at his touch, but he gently pulled her shoulder toward him. "You're not telling me something."

With a sigh, she faced him, and the sight drove the breath from his lungs as surely as a blow to the chest would have.

An angry red scrape marred her cheek, bits of dirt and gravel clinging to raw skin. A small cut wept at her eyebrow. Her fingers were streaked with red where she pressed them to her nose.

"Rachel." Each of those wounds looked painful. "Did he get a blow in?" The heated anger that surged through him bordered on irrational. Someone had harmed Rachel right in front of him. He fought to stop his feet from turning and blasting across the parking lot in a futile search for the man who'd done this. He deserved to be brought to justice.

Marshall pursed his lips and exhaled slowly. His anger wouldn't do Rachel any good at this moment. She needed his peace and his help more than she needed him to run off half-cocked.

No matter how much he needed to do something to make up for failing her.

"The nose was his doing. The rest I did to myself trying to get to him under the vehicle." She wouldn't look him in the eye. "My fault entirely."

"Let me see." He stepped closer, gripped her wrist lightly and drew her hand from her face. He was surprised she let him. "Lift your chin a little." When she did, he surveyed her features. While her nose was bloodied, there was no unnatural bend to the bridge and no telltale bruising beneath her eyes. "I don't think he broke it."

"That's good." She tried to pull back, but his firm grip on her wrist kept her close.

"I'm more worried about that cut by your eyebrow." He leaned closer. The cut was short, maybe a half inch long. It had almost stopped bleeding already, and it wasn't as deep as it had first appeared. While he'd initially thought she might have taken a good whack to the head, closer inspection revealed she'd likely caught a rock or a small piece of glass when she'd smashed her face into the ground while trying to get under the car. "I don't think it's as bad as it looks."

"Good." She backed away, tugging her wrist from his grasp.

The back of Marshall's neck heated. Until the space between them left cold air in her wake, he hadn't realized his face had been close enough to hers to feel the warmth of her breath. He swallowed what felt a little like embarrassment. "I have some napkins and a first-aid kit in the car. We'll get you cleaned up. You might want to go to the ER and let them take a look at—"

"I'm fine. It's a scrape. My fault."

My fault. She'd said those exact words more than once, and he wasn't about to let her walk away from him this afternoon with such a twisted idea on her conscience. If the truth were put out there, he was to blame for letting the guy get away, for not jumping in and helping her sooner. He should have known something like this was coming. "You didn't ask for this, and you didn't cause it, either. Now stand still for two minutes, and we'll fix that up."

She started to speak. No, she was about to argue, but Marshall held up his hand. "That's an order, *Lieutenant.*"

Her mouth twitched, but it was hard to tell whether the cause was amusement or frustration. Marshall ignored it, hoping she'd do as he'd asked. In the real world, he had no authority to issue an order to her, but the uniforms they both wore said he outranked her. He'd run with the illusion if he had to.

Rounding the vehicle, he dug the first-aid kit from under the back seat, grabbed a wad of napkins from the console and came back to her.

She leaned back against the passenger door with her arms crossed. When he held out the napkins, she took them and wiped sand and gravel off her hands. "Not my finest moment."

"Nobody could have foreseen someone hiding under my truck." Although, he should have expected it. Marshall laid the first-aid kit on the roof of her car, pulled on a pair of the gloves he found inside, then tore open a pack of disposable wet wipes. He pressed one into her hand. "This will help. Let me get your face."

"I can do it." She reached for the package of wipes, but he held them out of her reach.

"You want to reopen that cut while you're blundering around trying to be Captain Independent?"

She sighed and dropped her hand, sinking against the door. "This is so embarrassing."

Marshall forced a smile. "Stop arguing with the guy who's trying to make you presentable to the world." The situation was dire, and he wasn't ready to think about the implications of what had just happened, of why he was a target or of what this meant for his daughter. For the moment, Emma was safe at school and they were safe in this parking lot. He hoped.

This time, it was definitely a smile that twitched at the corner of her lip. "Yes, sir."

"Ma'am?" The voice came from the rear of their vehicles. "Are you okay?"

Both of them turned toward the sound. Marshall eased in front of her. Somebody had already injured her once. They wouldn't get another swing in without coming through him first.

A young military police officer narrowed his eyes as he leaned to the side to see around Marshall. He caught sight of Rachel's face, then rested his hand on the weapon at his hip. "Captain, I need you to step away from the lieutenant."

"What?" The guy had to be kidding him.

"Step away from the lieutenant." The MP spoke with more authority this time. His gaze flicked to something over Marshall's left shoulder.

Rachel grasped the back of his sleeve. "Captain Slater." She said the words as if she wanted his attention.

When he turned toward her, he saw why there was a tinge of concern in her voice. While the first MP had his attention at the front, another had flanked them, coming up between the cars behind them.

Already, the handful of folks moving in and out of the food court and the P/X had slowed, drawn by the presence of a military police vehicle, two MPs and a woman with a bloodied face.

All the air leaked from Marshall's lungs. Great. This looked incredibly bad to anyone watching.

He knew how this worked. Had seen the system move in multiple times on men in his chain of command, sometimes rightfully so. No matter what the truth was, he was already convicted in the minds of the bystanders and of the MPs.

"Sir." The second MP stepped closer, reaching for his handcuffs. "We received a call about a man matching your description assaulting a lieutenant matching hers. Please put your hands behind your back."

He didn't dare look at Rachel. It was best to obey and sort this out rather than escalate a confrontation.

But as he obeyed the MP's order, he glanced at the growing crowd, and there was no doubt—his reputation was already in tatters.

FIVE

Rachel wanted to jump between Marshall and the MP who was now wielding handcuffs, but sudden moves around men with their hands already poised on their weapons rarely ended well. She'd been in their shoes, had started her career as an MP. Being on the other side of the encounter was a whole new sensation.

Wisely choosing not to make waves, Marshall stood with his hands out to his sides, watching the MP instead of Rachel.

Her mind spun through options. It wasn't like she could pull out her own badge and tell them to back down. There were too many witnesses, and she'd come close enough to blowing her cover on Thursday night.

But she had to stop this. Marshall was a single father. If this went any further and public suspicion of any sort turned toward him, he could potentially find himself under scrutiny despite the truth.

Slowly, Rachel raised both hands as the MP reached to handcuff Marshall. A twinge in her shoulder let her know she had a few other injuries that hadn't yet reared their ugly heads, but she kept her expression neutral as she held her hands in view to avoid escalating the situation. She couldn't let this go any further. Once Marshall was in cuffs, his guilt would be solidified in the eyes of everyone watching, even though he was 100 percent innocent. One video or photo could spread across the internet like an out-of-control wildfire. Any whiff of scandal involving a soldier was sensational, and the eyes of social media saw what they wanted to see.

She glanced at the MP's rank and name. "Specialist Collier, if I may?" *Play the respect card.* It went a whole lot further than playing the rank card.

"Ma'am?" He paused, but only long enough to glance at her as he stepped closer to Marshall.

The skin around her mouth stung as she talked, but she didn't dare wince. The last thing she wanted was misplaced sympathy that would make them want to defend her against Marshall. "That call was wrong. I don't know who made it, but it was wrong."

This time, when Specialist Collier hesitated, he looked her full in the face. "You look banged up to me, ma'am."

"But he didn't do it. Captain Slater is my company commander. We were at the food court working over lunch." She had to tell the truth, but she had to do it delicately. "Someone was hiding under his car, and when we came out, that's who attacked me. The captain was merely helping."

The two MPs glanced at each other. Likely, they'd heard victims defend domestic violence perpetrators before. The typical operating procedure would be to handcuff Marshall and to separate them to prevent just such a misplaced defense.

His reputation was in her hands. "I know what you're thinking, but there are cameras all over this parking lot. You can view them. I have no reason to lie, not when that lie can be so easily checked." She dipped her chin toward the ground. "The captain's brake line has been tampered with." That should be all the proof their MPs needed, although it gave away a whole lot more than she wanted. There was no way to have his car repaired or towed without raising suspicion, though, so she might as well toss it all out there.

With a quick nod at the first MP, Specialist Collier backed up and dropped to one knee, peering under the vehicle. He reached out, touched something, then sniffed it. Brushing his fingers clean on the side of his leg, he stood and holstered his handcuffs. "You can relax, Captain." He rested his hands on the belt at his hips. "Why would someone do that to your vehicle?"

"I have no idea." Marshall sagged against the SUV beside Rachel and crossed his arms over his chest. He sounded weary. No doubt it had been stressful nearly being handcuffed in front of a small knot of onlookers. It was likely he was connecting the dots between the sabotage on the SUV and the attempted break-in at his house on Thursday evening.

Specialist Collier took Marshall's answer in stride, then walked around the vehicle to confer with his partner. The two MPs began to disperse the crowd.

Marshall watched them.

Rachel watched him. His jaw was tight. The lines around his eyes had deepened in the past few minutes. He looked like a man in need of a three-day sleep.

Like a man who was worried about his daughter's safety.

Rachel laid a hand on his forearm. His muscles were tight beneath her touch, giving away his tension as much as the stiff line of his shoulders did. "You okay?"

"No." He turned to face her, effectively dropping her hand from his arm. "Why is this happening?"

"I don't know."

Rachel lifted her hand to scratch an itch on her cheek, but Marshall grabbed her wrist before she could make contact. "Don't. You'll start it bleeding again. Or you'll get it infected since you had your hands on the ground earlier. Let me finish cleaning you up. I'm sure the MPs are nowhere near through with us, and you'd probably like to be squared away before they come back for a statement."

He was right. She'd almost forgotten she'd been injured. And taking care of her seemed to ease some of the anxiety in him. She opened the door and eased onto the seat, wincing as her shoulder gave another twinge.

Marshall's eyebrows drew together. "You're hurt somewhere else?"

"No." She lifted her face to him, although the height of the SUV had them at nearly eye level. "Just banged my shoulder into the ground when he hit me. Knocked me off balance. I promise it's just from the contact and it's not broken or anything."

She'd earned her stripes. She didn't need to be coddled just because she was a woman.

With a sigh, Marshall lightly gripped her chin with one hand and turned her face slightly. He brushed at her cheek with the wipe, recoiling when she flinched. "Sorry. You scraped it pretty good, but it won't scar unless you mess with it." He turned her face toward him and caught her eye. "You don't want that, do you?"

Their gaze held. The expression on his face, which had started with a slight teasing glint, turned almost tender. He was studying her almost as though something about her had changed in the past few minutes.

Something that telegraphed from him to her and lodged in her chest. Despite their location in a parking lot and the circumstances of his being so near, a zip ran along her spine.

Marshall's chin jerked as if he'd felt the same thing. But then he seemed to break free of his thoughts and turned her face away from him again.

Dark circles danced in front of her eyes. She wasn't breathing. Rachel tried to pull in a deep breath slowly so that he wouldn't notice, but the air shuddered somewhere between her nose and her chest. What was wrong with her? She was older than thirty. She shouldn't be getting schoolgirl, boy-band crush jitters over a fellow soldier.

Especially not when she was still undercover and the soldier was a man whom it seemed she was going to have to protect.

She managed a steadier breath as he began to wipe her cheek again. "So, you can tell you're a dad."

From the corner of her eye, she saw him smile.

Good. Whatever weird moment had been between them was officially broken. "Yeah. I've dealt with a lot of skinned elbows and knees. Bumped heads and bruises. I even survived a trip to the ER when Emma cut open her shin on a tree root while she was playing in the backyard with her cousins." He stopped wiping her face to inspect her scrape, intent on her wound. "Although, that one nearly killed me."

"I can imagine."

Reaching for the first-aid kit, he pulled on a clean glove and held up a small tube. "Antibiotic cream?"

"Why not?"

With his middle finger, he dabbed at her

skin and Rachel relaxed, letting him take care of her. It had been a long time since she'd let someone else take the reins, since she had trusted someone else to come close to her physical person or her emotions.

It almost felt like having a friend.

Marshall had stopped touching her and was staring at the tube in his hands.

"What's wrong?" She'd reach for him again, but she was sort of afraid to touch him at this point. The last thing she needed was a repeat zap to her system. Another one might do permanent damage.

"You never answered my question."

Yeah, she'd been afraid he'd come back around to his situation, to why this was happening to him. She leaned out of the vehicle to look toward the aisle, where the MPs had scattered the small crowd. The first MP strode toward the building, likely to look at the video feed. Specialist Collier was on his phone. He looked away when he saw her watching.

She reached for the tube of medicine, took the cap from his other hand and closed it, then pressed it into his palm. "I don't know what's going on." She lowered her voice and glanced around to make sure no one was close enough to hear her. "My team will look at the surveillance footage. I have backup coming in. Someone will have eyes on you at all times."

"Because you think this is about me."

"I know it's about you." She didn't want to scare him, but she also wasn't going to pull any punches. There was no denying it now, not with brake fluid spilled onto the asphalt. "You need to cancel those Christmas invitations. It's pretty clear now that somebody is out to hurt you."

Marshall walked into his kitchen and stared at the stainless-steel fridge. The couple of bites of steak sub he'd managed to down before all the drama at the P/X were long digested. He was hungry.

No, he was thirsty, and that was the worst of all.

He'd given up alcohol years ago but, staring at the fridge now, all he wanted was a cold beer.

Puffing out a breath, he jerked open the door and grabbed a citrus soda. The door had almost swung shut when he caught the handle, reached back in and retrieved another one. He probably wasn't the only one who needed an afternoon caffeine kick.

Walking across the slate tile floor, he

plunked one of the sodas on the natural wood table beside Rachel's computer, then went to stare out the window at the backyard. His SUV had been towed to the dealership and would be returned to him sometime this evening. It still didn't seem possible that someone had tampered with it. Things like this didn't happen to people like him, did they?

The rapid tapping of her fingers on the keyboard provided the only sound in the room. Rachel was coordinating something with her team, but she had yet to read him in. He probably didn't want to know, especially since someone had already passed word along to her that the P/X cameras had yielded no clues. While her attacker had been spotted, he'd kept his face away from the cameras. No help there.

It would soon be time to pick up Emma from school, and they'd hit the coffee shop drive-through for their weekly "coffee" date. For Em, that meant flavored frothed milk, a treat that made her feel so grown-up.

He smiled. Em loved anything she deemed to be *grown-up*, but she was still very much his little girl. Outside the window, her play set dominated the small fenced yard. Snow coated the elevated wood surfaces, but most of the white stuff was gone. They were due another storm in a few days that would likely give them a white Christmas.

He'd forgotten how temperamental Tennessee weather could be. About as temperamental as his own emotions right now. He cracked open the soda and took a long sip, hoping the caffeine would wipe some of the fog out of his brain. "Is it safe for Em to be around me?" The question came out before he considered it, the crux of his anxious thoughts.

The tapping stopped, and the silence hung heavily. There was a soft *pop* as Rachel opened her drink. He actually heard her swallow before she spoke. "Someone will be watching your house twenty-four hours a day. She'll be as safe here as she would be anywhere else unless the threat escalates."

He definitely didn't want to consider what *escalate* might mean. "I don't know how I did it, but somehow I've managed to put my daughter in danger." He pressed the side of his fist against the dark wood door frame, relishing the feel of the pressure against his flesh. Somehow, it cut through the fog in his mind and reminded him there was a real world outside his thoughts. That he was safe at home and Em soon would be, too.

He should have picked her up at school instead of letting her stay the rest of the day. But the truth was, Em was a routine-oriented little girl who didn't take well to change. It was best to keep her schedule as regular as possible, or she'd get anxious. And an Emma tantrum was a force of nature.

"You didn't do this to her." The chair scraped against the tile floor and Rachel stood beside him, her shoulder practically touching his. "You didn't put your daughter in danger. There's nothing to indicate that anyone wants to harm her. Don't be so hard on yourself."

"She's not in danger?" Marshall spun on one heel, and they were practically nose to nose. "Someone cut my brake line. What if you hadn't noticed? What if I'd decided to pick up Em from school? What if those brakes had failed at a red light?" He looked down at her, desperate for her to understand the anxiety raging through him. "I could have lost my daughter."

"But you didn't. And you won't."

The calm in her voice did nothing to slake his hot fear. "That man had a gun. You suspect he was coming after me, and my daughter was asleep on the couch beside me." His voice was low, hoarse. "What if you hadn't seen him?" The horrible, nightmarish images wouldn't stop running on a loop in his head.

"But I did." Rachel lifted a hand as though she was going to touch his arm, then dropped it and stepped away from him. "Do you believe in God?"

"Yes." Where was she going with this?

"Then trust He's got your back. That He's watching over you and Emma."

"Bad things still happen. You've seen it yourself." Soldiers died. Wives died. All manner of evil slipped in.

"You're right, but this is one of those times when we have to do our best and trust. Otherwise, fear will keep you awake at night."

Marshall jerked. She was hitting too close to home. If only fear had kept him awake on the night Maggie had died…

Rachel didn't seem to notice his guilt. "Your holiday leave started today and runs through the week after New Year's. You'll stay home as much as possible. It's a contained area. My teammate Thalia will be here soon, and she'll take turns with me keeping an eye on the place. There will never be a moment when you're alone or when someone isn't on point for you. And with the battalion practically empty, there's a high likelihood we'll put an end to this before Christmas Eve." She leaned forward just enough to catch his eye. "Marshall, I'm not letting anything happen to you or that baby girl of yours. I promise."

There was no way she could make that promise, but the conviction in her voice and the steel in her eye made him believe her.

It also made him feel incredibly foolish for coming unglued in front of her. "The last time I…" No. He couldn't tell her that story. Not yet. Maybe not ever.

He dragged his hand across his head and walked away, dropping into one of the wooden chairs at the kitchen table. He set his can in front of him and twisted it from side to side. It revealed too much of his failure.

From the door, Rachel watched him, then came back to sit in the chair she'd just vacated. "You know, you treat those soft drinks like you need them to survive. It's like you're addicted."

The words crashed like a tsunami. His fingers froze. "What?" How had she done that? Pegged him in a way no one else ever had? Guessed one of his darkest secrets just by looking at him?

"It's just something I noticed." She shoved the laptop aside and held her own soda between her hands on the table like it was a coffee mug. "I was married to a highly functioning alcoholic. Beer was his drink of choice. If he was stressed, it was the first thing he reached for. Kind of like you and the soda. You headed straight for the fridge the other night when I was here and again a few minutes ago, just like he used to when..." She sat back and flicked one hand in the air. "Know what? That's got nothing to do with anything."

Marshall pressed his thumb into the thin can, the aluminum giving way slightly beneath the pressure. He'd worked closely with this woman for three months. More than once he'd started to think of her as a friend, had found her easy to talk to and joke around with. But he'd always kept his professional distance, given that she was a woman and a subordinate in his chain of command.

It was also because something in him had always been slightly drawn to her, something that scared him more than a little.

Now everything had changed—a barrier had crumbled between them. For the first time since Maggie had died, he wanted to talk. There weren't many people he'd been able to open up to, but Rachel felt safe. It was likely because, one day soon, she'd wrap up her investigation and walk out his door for the last time, which meant no matter what he felt, he couldn't pursue it.

She would walk out carrying his secrets with her.

Picking up the can, he turned it and read the yellow-and-green label. "That was me."

"What was you?"

"I was a beer guy. Didn't matter the brand. Didn't matter the type." He plunked the can onto the table. "Two brutal deployments and waking up one day as a widower with a small child can really mess with your head."

"I'm sorry."

He waved his hand in a downward motion. He didn't want the pity. He'd got his fill of it in the wake of Maggie's death.

Nobody seemed to understand that it had all been his fault. Their pity was misplaced.

"Emma was only two when her mom died. It was just me and her. After she'd go to bed at night, I headed for the fridge. It started to happen more and more. A lot of my money went to self-medicating myself into sleep every night."

"You're not the only one."

"Your ex?"

She turned her attention to her computer screen and nodded once, a thin lock of her brown hair brushing across her cheek.

"How long were you married?" She was fiercely independent and, although friendly, a bit of a loner, though that was probably due more to the job than to her personality. He simply couldn't picture her with a husband.

Maybe because he didn't want to.

"A little more than a year, and it's been over for several years. We were both looking for stability after a rough deployment. I looked for comfort in him. He looked for it in a bottle and in women who weren't me." She said it so matter-of-factly, as if she were rattling off the weather forecast before a static-line jump.

He wanted to catch her eye, to offer some sympathy, but she never looked up from her computer.

"Staff Sergeant Thalia Renner will be here in less than two hours." She quickly typed something. "And you shouldn't feel sorry for me, if that's what you're thinking. I'm fine. So are you."

That was debatable.

"There are a lot of soldiers who dive into the bottle. A few of them come out of it. You clearly did."

"Because I'm Emma's only parent." He flicked the top of the can. Now that he'd uncorked the bottle on his story and heard hers, he wasn't ready to stop talking. "One night, I was on beer three, watching the news, and there was this story about a cop who saved a choking baby. It whacked me between the eyes. What if something happened to Em and I couldn't get her to the hospital? Or I didn't wake up? I'm her first line of defense. It broke me right in two. She needed me, and I was failing her." He wouldn't fail that precious little girl the way he'd failed her mother. "I poured it all out that night." He lifted the can of soda in a mock salute, tipping it toward her. "Maybe it's wrong, but caffeine took its place."

"The lesser of two evils?"

"Maybe. Speaking of evil." Marshall shoved his drink away with three fingers. "I hate looking at my soldiers with suspicion. Somebody under my company's roof is selling out our country. You know what that does to morale, right?"

"That's one of the reasons this is under wraps."

"I've been so concerned with Emma being safe, I haven't had time to think about who our bad actor may be. A few people come to mind as possibilities, but I hate to—" His phone vibrated on the table, and he leaned forward to look at it, then picked it up and frowned. "Em's school. Hang on."

He answered, and a businesslike voice responded. "Captain Slater, we need you at school. There's an issue with Emma."

SIX

"Where's my daughter?" Marshall shoved through the front door of the school as soon as the remote lock buzzed. He swiped his black beret from his head in an automatic motion that Rachel imitated as she stepped through behind him, pocketing her car keys.

His words were a hollow echo in the empty space. While a handful of cars already waited out front in the car pickup line, no one was in the entryway between the exterior and interior glass doors. The cheery red, white and green Christmas decorations taped to the windows were a striking contrast to Marshall's frenzied urgency. He was still wearing his uniform, and he cut an imposing figure. Fear and concern emanated from him in waves that were a little too much like anger.

Even though Rachel was quite used to seeing him in uniform and in command mode, his tilted emotional balance rocked her. He needed to take a deep breath and pull it together or this would not go well with the staff waiting inside. She reached for his arm as he pushed the lever on the interior door. "Marshall, wait."

For a moment, it seemed he was going to keep marching forward, but he froze with the door half-open, one foot poised to step through. He didn't turn, but at least she had his attention and he had slowed down a little.

She stepped closer until she was almost standing against his back and lowered her voice. "Emma is in there, and she'll be watching you, as will the other children, who are going to be headed home soon. None of them need to see Emma's daddy fly through those doors like an angry avenger. If you don't want to cause a scene, then you need to pause and take a deep breath. And remember, she's not in danger at the moment." The emergency centered around a phone call made to the school, a claim that Marshall had been in an accident and that Emma would be picked up by someone else.

He inhaled sharply, probably about to argue, but then he held the breath before gradually releasing it. "You're right." His shoulders lifted and lowered with another slow inhalation and exhalation. "If Em is in the office, I need to be careful. She's too young to remember what happened to her mother, but she can get a bit anxious if her world isn't in order. I think she carries some emotional memory from that time." He looked over his shoulder at her. "Being a nanny taught you well."

He was walking again before she could answer.

It was just as well. His brown eyes that close to hers had given her a little jolt that she definitely didn't need to feel again. She'd already shared too much with him today. That little tidbit about her marriage to Robert had slipped through the barricade before she'd even realized it had escaped. Her past was none of Marshall's concern, even if the fact that he used to share the same vice as her ex left her more than a little concerned herself.

But this wasn't about her, and it certainly wasn't personal. Her job was to be quiet and find evidence. Nothing more.

Rachel stepped through the door Marshall held for her, then followed a few paces behind him, opting to play the role of supportive friend while they were in the school.

Although, it was doubtful the school staff would see it quite that way. They likely all knew that Marshall was a widower. Given his all-American soldier good looks and the way his uniform fit like it had been cut just for him, it was even more likely that several of the single room moms or young teachers had set their eyes on Emma's father. A female soldier like Rachel joining him on campus after the kind of phone call he'd received was likely to set all kinds of scuttlebutt into motion before their car even made it out of the parking lot.

Oh well. It wasn't ideal, but it might be better to let everyone gossip. It would stop them from ever suspecting that she was here on a mission.

With the students preparing to leave for Christmas vacation, the school hallway was jovial and noisy. From around the corner, excited voices and laughter sounded as students prepared to leave for the day.

At the main office, Marshall held the door open for her, then stepped around her to the desk. The middle-aged man at the counter looked from Marshall to Rachel and back again, the suspicion Rachel had just been contemplating alive in his expression.

Before he could speak, Marshall jump-started the conversation. "Where's Emma?"

"Good afternoon, Captain Slater. She's in her classroom, and she's perfectly safe. We haven't let her know anything. Our school resource officer is there as well, just in case."

As Marshall pivoted on one heel to head down the hall after his daughter, the man spoke again. "Before you go, the principal wants to talk to you without Emma present. There's no need to upset her."

From where she stood between Marshall and the hallway door, Rachel could see his jaw tense and his nostrils flare. He wanted his daughter, wanted to see for himself that she was safe. Delay was not his friend.

But the school's greeter had a point.

Marshall's gaze met Rachel's, and he seemed to draw something from her that reset his stance. From the shift in his expression, he'd managed to dig up his thought-driven soldier and let it overtake his emotion-driven father. Likely, it wouldn't last long.

"Okay." When he turned back to the counter, his voice was deeper and stronger, but his hand still shook slightly as he shoved his beret into his uniform's leg pocket.

Rachel's heart went out to him. He wouldn't calm down until he saw his daughter.

"This way." The greeter raised part of the counter and stepped aside for Marshall to pass through.

Rachel glanced around the brightly decorated space and found a small grouping of chairs near the door. She headed for a blue plastic seat next to a table littered with school brochures and local magazines. He'd fill her in on what was happening when he came out.

But he turned as the greeter fell into line behind him. "You're coming, aren't you? I need you in there."

The greeter's eyebrow arched. Well, there was another tip of the gasoline can to add to that burning fire of gossip. *Did you see that woman with Captain Slater? How did a girl like her manage to land him?*

She wanted to face-palm her forehead. Would her high school insecurities never fully go away? She was a soldier, a captain in the United States Army. Shouldn't she be above caring what other people thought of her?

She should, but she was also still a woman. A woman whose husband had chosen multiple other women over her.

Besides, she hadn't *landed* Marshall. As he stepped to the side and let her pass him into the principal's office, she was careful not to let her shoulder brush his chest. She was here as an investigator, definitely not as a woman.

The principal stood and shoved aside a stack of Christmas cards as they entered, and she indicated they should sit in the seats in front of her desk, sitting when they did. She cast a quick, questioning glance at Rachel. "I'm Mrs. Rebecca Stratton."

"Rachel Shelby." The undercover alias rolled off her tongue with practiced precision.

"She's a friend." Marshall stepped in, clearly eager to get to his daughter. "What happened?"

Mrs. Stratton reached for an orange sheet of paper on the corner of her desk, which was stacked with gift bags and wrapped boxes. She was clearly a favorite with her students.

"I just wanted to make sure you have all the details of what happened, although Emma was never in direct danger." She scanned the paper, then passed it to Marshall, who watched her instead of reading it. "Shortly before we phoned you, the school received a call. The caller was a man who stated that you had been in an accident and that someone else would be picking up Emma from school today. As you know, we have code words for instances when someone who is not on the approved list will be picking up a child. He didn't know the word. In fact, he laughed when we asked and hung up on our secretary."

"Do you know who it was? Have you

called the police?" The orange paper crumpled in Marshall's grip, and Rachel fought the urge to reach over and lay a hand on his arm. He didn't need her adding fuel to the rumors.

"We have no idea who the man was." Mrs. Stratton tipped her chin toward the paper Marshall held. "That's our incident report. With your blessing, we can have the police trace the number that came up on our caller ID."

Rachel leaned forward, then checked herself. She needed that number, but there was no way to get it without tipping her hand.

"I want that phone number." Marshall almost seemed to read her mind.

"I can't do that. The police have given us specific instructions in these situations."

Before Marshall could react, Rachel laid a hand on his wrist. Mrs. Stratton was right. As much as they all wanted access to the school's caller ID, she couldn't hand the number over to just anybody. No amount of wishing or talking was going to change the law.

Mrs. Stratton rested her folded hands on her desk and leaned forward. "Captain Slater, can you think of anyone who would do this? Typically in these situations, there's a custody dispute of some sort, and the noncustodial parent is making an attempt to get to the child. There's no flag in Emma's file, and I know your situation would preclude that, but I need to ask."

Marshall shook his head. "No. But I'm going to find out." He stood abruptly, the incident report twisted in his hands. "I'll see my daughter now, ma'am."

There was nothing else to say.

Rachel stood with Marshall and glanced at the telephone on the principal's desk. Eagle Overwatch had a phenomenal technical genius in Dana Richardson. Maybe she could find a way to access the school's telephone system and get that number. This wasn't the CIA or a top secret facility. They couldn't be that sophisticated.

And that number was a crucial piece of evidence in her case. If their thief had decided to target Marshall, caller ID might lead them straight to him, putting a close to her case and an end to any threats against the Slaters.

Following Marshall and Mrs. Stratton from the office and into the hallway, Rachel kept her gaze on the back of Marshall's head. There was still no chatter that intel had been able to ferret out, no indication why their bad guy would suddenly want to get to Marshall. She had a feeling that if she could solve that mystery, she'd know the perpetrator's identity.

But could she figure it out before Marshall and Emma paid the ultimate price?

"So do you think you can make that happen?" Rachel upped the volume on her phone and laid it in the middle of the small, square wood table in the corner of the studio apartment over the detached garage in Marshall's backyard.

Across from her, Staff Sergeant Thalia Renner sat with her elbows braced on the table, watching the phone. Her dark hair was up in a ponytail, and she was dressed in black, ready for a night in the chilly December air, watching the Slater house while Rachel tried to catch some much-needed rest.

Rachel's other team member, Staff Sergeant Phillip Campbell, was in the house talking to Marshall and his father-in-law, who had arrived only a few minutes earlier. According to Marshall, Maggie's father was a retired army ranger who wouldn't take no for an answer when he learned his granddaughter had been targeted.

Although it indicated that the situation was beginning to skid, Rachel was relieved to have her team present. It felt good not to have to go it alone any longer.

The phone was silent except for a few random clicks, evidence that their tech consultant, Dana Richardson, was combing through her ever-present laptop and its endless number of what her husband referred to as "tech toys." If there was a way to get to that phone number on the school's system, Dana would find it.

"Here's the thing." Dana's voice was muffled, probably because she was speaking through the wireless earpiece she wore constantly. "I can get the right permissions from higher to hack into the system. That shouldn't be a problem from a legal standpoint. And with it being a school, I doubt there's much more than a basic firewall in place. I'm fairly certain I can get into the phone system. But have you ever been in an elementary school office? The phones ring constantly. I can get you a list of numbers that correspond to the ten- or fifteen-minute time period before Captain Slater received the call about his daughter, but I can't pinpoint exactly which one was our bad guy. It will take me some time to match phone numbers to known school contacts and vendors and eliminate them from suspicion."

"Not only that—" Thalia sat back and tugged her ponytail tighter "—but the likelihood of the phone he used to call the school being a burner is really high. If our guy's smart, he dialed and dumped. I know that's what I'd do."

"Hopefully our guy isn't that intelligent," Rachel muttered. She held up a hand to stop Thalia from speaking. "I know, I know. He's already kept me guessing for months and has managed to walk out of the battalion with half a dozen or more hard drives, so he's likely smarter than the average criminal." Her failure to take him down indicated he was either cunning or had things coincidentally go his way often enough to keep his identity hidden.

Thalia tapped the tip of her nose. Rachel had nailed what they were all thinking.

Rachel slouched in the seat. "Right now, this is all we have to go on." She was too tired to work up coherent thoughts for much longer. "Let me know if you find anything."

"You've got it." From her desk at her home in Mountain Springs, North Carolina, Dana sounded almost chipper. Probably because she was about to go have hot chocolate or coffee in her log cabin living room with the giant Christmas tree her brand-new husband had put up. "Get some rest, Rach. You burn the candle at both ends much longer, and you're going to be no good to anybody."

She knew. Boy, did she know. "Out." Rachel punched the end button on the phone, then spun it in the middle of the table like a top. Everything about this investigation felt like one step forward and three back.

"She's right, you know." Thalia pressed an index finger square into the face of the phone to stop the spinning. "You can't run on coffee forever."

Though she'd only been with Eagle Overwatch for about eight months, Thalia had proved to be a valuable member of the unit. She was intelligent and levelheaded and had been Rachel's first choice when she'd been given command of her own team earlier in the year. Like Rachel, Thalia was a former military police officer who'd seen her own share of pain but was stronger and more tactically minded for it. At the moment, Rachel wouldn't want anyone else at her side. While Phillip was a competent team member and one of the best men Rachel knew, he'd never understand the female point of view the way Thalia did.

Pocketing her phone, Rachel glanced at the small kitchenette. The warm wood cabinets and sophisticated gray walls echoed the feel of the rest of the small studio apartment, which would probably feel like a retreat under other circumstances. A coffeepot sat cold and empty on the dark granite counter. She could brew a pot and suck it dry, but that wouldn't help her sleep tonight. What she needed was real rest, not the artificial punch of energy that caffeine provided.

But she couldn't sleep yet. She got up and walked over to the counter, grabbed a piece of the pizza that Phillip had brought up half an hour earlier, then dropped back into her seat at the table. It was only five, but the two bites of rice she'd managed at the food court earlier were long gone.

Wow. That felt like weeks ago.

"What are you thinking?" Thalia grabbed her own piece of pizza, then flopped onto the sofa that sat at a right angle to the table, facing a small TV. Behind her, a queen-size bed with a red comforter waited beside a heavy wooden nightstand. It was a comfortable, cozy little space normally reserved for Marshall's father when he came into town.

Now it was rapidly becoming home base for their investigation.

Rachel swallowed pepperoni and cheese. "You want to know what I'm thinking?" She washed down the pizza with a huge swig of water. "Why? Why is our bad guy changing up his game? That's what I'm thinking."

"You mean why are they coming after Captain Slater?" Though she'd left Boston as a young child, Thalia's *r*'s were still slightly muted. When people initially met her, they couldn't quite place where she was from. It was a running joke with everyone who knew her, one that she seemed to enjoy.

"I'm missing something." Of course she was. She'd been here three months and should have easily apprehended the thief by now. Sure, the case was complicated because the thefts were random, but still... The fact that she was failing robbed Rachel of her appetite. She got up and tossed the rest of her pizza into the trash, then leaned against the kitchenette counter, bracing her palms on the granite behind her. "I doubt Phillip is going to get much new information out of Marshall tonight. He was done talking once we got Emma home and settled. He probably won't take his eyes off her for a while. I think there's a living room campout and a Christmas movie marathon on tap tonight, just because he can't bear to send her to her room alone."

"You think the threat against the daughter is viable?"

"I don't know. The way the principal described the incident, it's almost like the guy wanted to toy with Marshall's sense of security." Rachel sniffed and shoved away the warm image of family movie night. She needed to focus. "Then again, someone was at his house. They cut his brake line. Whether they were actually trying to take Emma or they just wanted to scare Marshall is up in the air."

"Marshall?" Thalia popped the last bite of pizza crust into her mouth and swiped her hands together. "We're on a first-name basis now?"

Rachel shot her a withering look. What she called the company commander was irrelevant. "The only thing I can figure is that he knows something, but he doesn't realize that it's important. I'm going to sit down with him tomorrow after we've both had a chance to rest and walk him through it. It's possible he saw something and he simply hasn't put it together yet. Either way, he has somebody scared enough to try to scare him."

"And you're sure no one's onto you?"

"There's not been a single threat in my direction. Although, me moving into the garage apartment might be a tip-off." Marshall had leaked word that her apartment was being treated for mold. Likely, some of the soldiers suspected there was more to it than that, but they probably also believed the two were secretly dating, if they thought about it at all.

Thalia stood, checked her hip for her SIG, then pulled her navy blue T-shirt down to cover it. Reaching for her jacket, she shrugged into the windbreaker and pocketed her phone. "Well, it's dark, so I'm going to head out and take up watch. I'm thinking the tree house at the back corner of the lot is a great place to start. Phillip will go back to your place for some sleep after he's done here and will take over around two." She strode for the door and stopped with her hand on the knob. "Based on the number of toys in the yard, I'm thinking Captain Slater spoils that little girl of his rotten." She grinned, then disappeared into the chilly night.

Rachel smiled. He probably did, but she couldn't blame him. She'd read the file Major Harrison had put together on the Slaters. Maggie Slater had died by suicide when Emma was barely two. Marshall had been the one to find his wife, according to the police report. His daughter was his whole world, all that he had left of the woman he'd lost.

Rachel yawned. It was early, but her Friday had started a couple of days ago with only a few catnaps here and there. She was toast. She fired off a quick text to Marshall and to Phillip to let them know that Thalia was on duty, then shut off the lights and collapsed on the bed in her sweats and a tee, way past caring about pajamas or face wash.

She awoke to stillness and the hot, sticky feeling of sleeping in her clothes. It was too quiet. She jolted straight up in the bed with the eerie feeling that someone was watching her. Pressing her hand to her chest to convince her heart to slow, Rachel swung her legs over the side of the bed, listening. Dim light filtered through the blinds, making every shadow look like a hulking ogre. Whatever had awakened her must have been in her imagination or magnified by the silence of sleep.

She glanced at the clock. Just after one. There was plenty of night left.

Sleep clung to her like a heavy blanket, and she was definitely ready for more. Standing, Rachel turned and pulled back the covers to climb into the bed properly.

The floor behind her creaked.

A weight slammed her face-first onto the bed, pinning her awkwardly at the waist. She struggled and fought, managing to get out only a small cry before a hand pressed the back of her head, shoving her face roughly into the thick downy mattress cover. Hard, stinging electric pain jolted from her already-wounded nose and cheek.

She fought for air. Couldn't gasp. Couldn't scream. There was only fabric and pain.

The weight shifted, moving forward, impossibly heavier on her head.

Rachel clawed desperately at the sheets, trying to push herself up, to make space for air, but the force holding her down was too heavy, had too much leverage. She couldn't buck, couldn't fight. Could hardly form a coherent thought. A high-pitched whine started in her head as oxygen rapidly depleted.

The weight moved slightly, and warm breath brushed her ear. A voice, low and harsh, ground against her hearing. "Slater is close to you. He likes you. Maybe loves you. He'll pay for what he did to me with your life."

SEVEN

Her strength ebbed as her lungs ached for air. Rachel had to change tactics before she lost consciousness. She couldn't lift herself against the weight.

But she could fight with what little reserves she had. Reaching behind her, she grabbed desperately at the hands against the back of her head, fingers landing on leather gloves. Clawing up, she found skin between the gloves and shirt cuff. Rachel dug her nails in as deeply as she could, dragging toward her with all the strength she had left.

The man roared and cursed, jerking away from the pain.

That slight release was all the leverage that Rachel needed. Lifting her head enough to gasp fresh air, she took full advantage of her adversary's pain. She shoved her palms into the bed and threw herself backward with all her weight and strength.

Her sudden movement threw her attacker off balance and knocked him to the floor. He dragged the bedside table and its contents along with him. The clatter was loud in the silence.

Still heaving air to replace the oxygen she'd lost, Rachel whirled and prepared to fight as the shadowed figure scrambled to his feet.

A shout from downstairs sent the man running before they could square off. He tripped over the edge of the couch in the darkness, nearly tumbling to the floor. He kept up momentum and stumbled to the door. His feet pounded on the stairs as another shout came from closer to the house.

Thalia was in pursuit.

Shaking with residual fear and adrenaline, Rachel ran for the door. From her vantage point on the second story, she watched the taillights of a dark pickup truck skid around the corner, too far away to see the license plate.

She slumped against the door frame, legs quaking and hands shaking. Her knees were water. The winter Tennessee air braced her lungs and cleared the fog from her mind faster than she'd imagined possible.

What had just happened?

The whole incident, from being jerked from a sound sleep to the perpetrator fleeing out the door, had likely lasted less than two minutes. Her brain rewound the scene and played it in slow motion again and again, drawing it out into hours, even days.

"Rach?" Thalia jogged through the open privacy gate and headed for the stairs.

The back door to the house opened, and Marshall ran out into the pool of light from the porch lamp, a pistol held low in both hands. He looked from Thalia in the yard to Rachel standing in the doorway. "Is everyone okay?"

"Emma?" Rachel needed to know the little girl was safe. She cast a quick prayer toward heaven. *Please let her have slept through the commotion.*

"She's asleep. Her grandfather is inside with her." Marshall holstered his weapon and descended the deck steps at a rapid clip, meeting Thalia at the foot of the garage stairs.

The two of them headed up together, with Thalia in the lead. She stopped in front of Rachel. "You okay?"

"What happened?" Marshall crowded close behind Thalia, his question tripping over hers.

As Thalia squeezed past her, on shaking

knees Rachel leaned more heavily against the door. With the adrenaline wearing off, her emotions were kicking in. She'd been close to death before, but it had never been personal.

As Marshall stepped up onto the small landing, her eyes locked with his. Somebody had wanted her dead because they were trying to hurt Marshall, which meant they viewed him as a threat.

And they viewed her as someone special to him.

At least her cover hadn't been blown.

His lips tight, he stared at her for a long moment before he gestured for her to enter the apartment ahead of him.

As soon as Rachel stepped away from the door, her knees gave out. Only Marshall's quick reflexes saved her. His arms were around her, and she was against his chest before she even realized what had happened.

He looked down, nearly nose to nose with her. "You are not okay." His voice was low and gravelly, filled with an emotion Rachel wasn't prepared to unpack.

Thalia flipped on the overhead light in the living area, banishing the darkness.

Breaking eye contact, Marshall drew away, keeping one arm around Rachel's waist as he guided her to the couch.

She eased down, willing her body to stop shaking.

"Drink this." Thalia met them at the couch and held out a glass of water. "Your face is red and raw again, and you're more jiggly than a jellyfish."

"It's adrenaline. That's it. The guy woke me up out of a deep sleep. Surprised me. I'll be fine." Still, she reached for the glass, her throat hot and raw from the fight for air.

Jerking away the glass before Rachel could take it, Thalia grabbed her wrist. "What's this?" She settled the glass on the coffee table as Marshall righted the end table, then sat beside Rachel on the couch.

Rachel stared at her hand as Thalia held it between them. Her fingernails were bloody, and a couple were packed with something...

With skin. She jerked her head up and looked straight at Thalia, the terrified victim in her soul giving way to the competent investigator in her mind. "That's DNA. I managed to tear up his arms."

"Whose arms?" Marshall sat forward and tried to force her to look at him. "What happened up here?"

Rachel ignored him and kept her focus on the job at hand. They had to collect the material from under her nails before it was contaminated. She addressed Thalia instead. "You have a collection kit?"

"In my bag." Thalia released her arm, headed for her duffel and came back with a sealed evidence collection kit. In short order, she'd scraped the material from beneath Rachel's nails and sealed it, then directed Rachel to clean up.

On shaky legs, Rachel crossed to the bathroom and obeyed, trying to scrub away not only the blood but the sensation from her fingertips. She could still feel hot breath on her cheek and the weight of death between her shoulder blades. Shutting off the water, she dried her hands, keeping her chin dipped to avoid the mirror. All she'd see looking back at her was failure. The victim. The one who messed up yet again.

All that had to be set aside. There was work to do if she wanted to make this right. The first order of business was to figure out who had attacked her. The second was to figure out why they viewed Marshall as a threat. Those two things would direct the course of the rest of her team's investigation.

She walked out of the bathroom with a renewed sense of self and purpose, keeping her eyes away from the bed where she'd nearly died. The inner strength she'd relied on so often on deployment would serve her well now.

So would the hefty prayers she was silently screaming.

Rachel leaned against the kitchen counter the same way she had earlier, as far from Marshall as she could possibly get. He complicated her thinking, and she needed a clear head.

"Someone was in the apartment?" He stood before she could relax against the granite. "They came directly after you?"

So he'd talked with Thalia while she was in the bathroom? She never should have left the room. She'd kind of hoped to keep that information between herself and Thalia, to let Marshall believe he'd heard nothing more than a false alarm.

Thalia wouldn't look at her. They'd have words later about her handing out information without consent from her team leader.

"It's fine." Rachel turned her attention back to Marshall, who stood by the couch with a stance that said he was prepared to run straight out the door to hunt down whoever had dared to come onto his property. "He woke me up and we fought. I won. And he made a fatal mistake." She held her freshly washed fingers up between them. "We now have DNA. If he really is a soldier, we may be able to have it run against the DNA database, since we're looking at someone selling hard drives containing sensitive intel."

"Speaking of that…" Thalia stepped in before Marshall could speak. "I can put the call in to Major Harrison to get the legal side rolling. But how do we want to get the kit tested? It's a solid six-hour drive back to HQ to put it into the hands of our lab geniuses."

"We need to keep this in-house as much as possible, and we need to get it there fast." Rachel dragged her hands down her face. "Go ahead and call Major Harrison. Have him send someone to meet one of us halfway. Or, if things go our way, there might be a helo running between Fort Campbell and Camp McGee in the next twelve hours that one of us could hitch a ride on."

"Or we could find a pilot who needs some flight hours."

"Bingo." Either way, they needed to get that DNA to their lab as soon as possible. Her entire investigation could be wrapped up with that sample if the courts gave them access to the armed forces database.

This was her biggest break yet. She'd focus on that instead of on the burning in her lungs and in her face.

"Now that we've got that all figured out..." Marshall rounded the couch and stood between the two women. Once again, he'd reached the limit of his patience and was ready for answers. "What happened out here?"

How much to say? Marshall deserved to know everything, but Rachel wasn't comfortable with telling him how close to death she'd come. She wasn't even ready to discuss that with Thalia. If word got back to Major Harrison, he might pull her entire team off the investigation, and that would leave Marshall with no cover at all.

She searched the ceiling for a balanced answer. Sensing Marshall wasn't going to wait much longer, Rachel finally spun out the basic story. "A man broke into the apartment. Thalia and I chased him off."

Thalia stood taller. "I missed him coming in. I had walked around the front of the house to find a better vantage point. It never occurred to me to keep an eye on the garage. I never thought you'd be a target. Either he knows we're investigating, or he coincidentally walked up at the most opportune moment imaginable. We may have blown our shot at keeping this under wraps."

"He's not targeting us. I doubt he even

knew you were out there." There were bigger things at play here, and they involved Marshall, not the team.

"You say that with an awful lot of confidence." Marshall closed the distance between them and stood just a couple of feet away. He watched her face in a way that said he could almost read what she wasn't saying. "How do you know?"

The question brought back the harsh whisper, the threat, the fear. It dragged out the words she really didn't want to say. "Because he thinks I mean something to you. And he wants to cause you pain."

Marshall jerked a chair away from the small kitchen table and dropped heavily into it, burying his head into his hands. The slight swirled texture in the light gray carpet did nothing for the nausea that was about to swamp him.

Someone wanted to hurt him, and they'd come after Rachel to do it. One of his soldiers must have interpreted the happenings of the past few days as proof that he and Rachel were seeing each other, and they'd targeted her, likely because they thought she was isolated and alone in the garage studio apartment. If this was run-of-the-mill revenge, they'd simply report him for suspicion of fraternization with a subordinate in his chain of command. This was worse. It was intensely personal.

This was why they'd called the school, as well. Whoever it was had found they couldn't get to Emma, so they'd gone to the next source.

Which meant Emma was still in danger.

Because he was her father.

How had this become so personal? The hatred directed at him seemed to swirl in the air, vile and rancid.

He dug his fingers into the sides of his head, trying to get his mind to focus on a plan. His daughter was in the crosshairs of a sadistic thief, and Marshall not only had no idea who, he had no idea why.

Rachel knelt in front of him. "We're going to find who's behind this."

Snapping to attention, he glared down at her. "When? How long before he slips past you again and goes too far?"

She winced but offered nothing further.

A few feet away, Thalia slipped between the couch and the table. "I'm going to head outside. Call the major. Wait for Phillip. Keep an eye on the house."

The door clipped shut behind her, but Marshall never bothered to look her way. It was Rachel he was the most concerned about in this room. Rachel in front of him and his daughter in the house.

For the first time, he got an up-close look at Rachel's face. Her forehead, nose and chin were red, as though she'd scrubbed them hard with a washcloth. Her cheek, already raw from the afternoon's crash into the pavement, was in even worse condition than before, the scabs rubbed away and weeping slightly.

There was something she wasn't telling him. Her face spoke of a bigger story than the words she'd so flippantly tossed at him a few minutes earlier.

He glanced around the apartment, piecing together the truth. He'd righted the end table that someone had knocked over. In the sleeping area, the nightstand was on its side, the contents scattered over a wide area between the bed and the bathroom door as if it had been violently thrown.

Marshall narrowed his eyes. That was where the fight had happened. And from the looks of things...

His gaze flew to Rachel's face, the film coming into focus. "He tried to suffocate you."

"It's not worth discussing."

"It most certainly is." He cupped her chin in his palms and let his fingers lie lightly along her jawline, turning her face so he could see the damage to her already-wounded cheek. The skin beneath her ear was soft and warm beneath his fingertips. Forget the fact that she was supposed to be protecting him. Right now, he wanted nothing more than to pull her to his chest, wrap his arms around her and stand between her and whoever had done this. To stop it from happening again. To gather Rachel and Emma and fly them to the far corners of the earth. "He hurt you." The words scraped out of his throat over what felt like sand and gravel.

When he shifted his gaze from her cheek to her eyes, they were bright with a sudden sheen of tears.

She inhaled sharply.

That gasp was the outward sound of the same blow that rocked his breathing. It was the knowledge that, just like he'd lay down his life to protect his daughter, he'd go to the ends of the earth to protect this woman.

Tired of thinking, Marshall wanted to feel. He let one thumb brush her lower lip, only breaking their gaze to follow the motion with his eyes.

Rachel's lips parted slightly.

The realization was a flash of lightning. She wanted him to kiss her.

There was no way he couldn't. No way he wouldn't. For the first time in years, the fire in his heart flared under a new flame.

Rachel jerked her head back and stood abruptly, turning away from him. She crossed her arms in front of her and stared at the door Thalia had vacated. "I'm a big girl, Marshall. I can take care of myself and of you. This is what I do. It's my job. I need you to worry about your daughter and let me worry about the rest. You have no need to concern yourself with what happens to me."

The words were ice, a cold knife to the heart.

A needed reminder of reality. He'd been about to kiss a woman who was investigating his soldiers. A woman who would be on her way out of his life as soon as she closed this case.

He'd been about to kiss a woman when he knew he was no good for any woman. When he couldn't save or protect...

When his daughter needed to be his sole focus so he wouldn't fail her.

His daughter, who was likely in danger because of her proximity to him.

He slumped into the chair and stared at the

ceiling, the wooden slats digging between his shoulder blades. He ought to apologize to Rachel, but to do so would be to admit what he'd been about to do, and neither of them needed that truth weighting the air between them. "What do we do now?"

"I want to send you and Emma away." She didn't move. Her back was a rigid wall.

Marshall opened his mouth to argue, but it wouldn't get him anywhere. She'd made up her mind.

And she was right. Em didn't need to be here, not while someone had proved tonight that they could gain access to the people he cared about before anyone was even aware he was there.

Her shoulders rose and lowered as she breathed deeply. "I'm going to send Phillip back to Camp McGee with the DNA, and I'm going to send Thalia with you and Emma to a safe house."

"A safe house?" He rose slowly, feeling every one of his thirty-two years and two combat tours.

"We have several options, but the one I'm thinking of is larger, away from things. You can take your family if they agree to remain there for the duration. Tell Emma it's a Christmas vacation. If it's snowed there this week, it will practically be a wonderland."

"It's less than a week until Christmas." Despite the circumstances, he couldn't fathom not waking up in his home on Christmas morning as his daughter raced down the stairs. Tomorrow was tree-decorating day. Maggie's father would help. Em had looked forward to it all year.

All that had to go away to ensure her safety.

With Phillip and Thalia gone, it would also leave Rachel here alone. "You need backup."

"I'll be fine."

There was something else under the words, but it was hard to discern if the emotion was fear or pride. She believed she could do this alone.

She probably could.

Marshall walked to the window by the TV and pulled down a slat in the blinds, staring at the closed curtains of his daughter's room above the kitchen. She was everything he lived for, and she was growing up without her mother because Marshall had failed Maggie. Because he'd stood down when he should have stood up.

If he ran now... If he left Rachel here and something happened to her, then he'd failed again. She needed him, whether she realized it or not. The company was his. The soldiers were his. He knew each one of them like they were family—or at least he thought he did. Her search for evidence would go so much faster if he were at her side. "Tonight's DNA evidence is only going to prove the identity of the person who attacked you here."

She remained motionless and silent.

"You're still going to need proof from the company to link that person to the theft of those hard drives. You're still going to need a way to build links in the chain from theft to seller if they aren't the same person. You could still be dealing with more than one person." He prayed for wisdom. What was the right thing to do? Either way, he was making someone he cared about walk this walk without him.

He knew what he had to do, knew what God was calling him to do, even though obedience to the call ripped his heart in two.

He swallowed and drew on the soldier in him, the one who had packed up shortly after Emma was born and deployed to serve his country overseas. He'd had to trust that his tiny baby girl would be safe then.

He'd have to trust God that she'd be safe

now, because even though this wasn't an overseas deployment, it was a call to action.

"You need me." He held up his hand to stop her from speaking, even though she wasn't facing him. "I'll send Emma into hiding with Maggie's dad, but I'm staying here with you." Saying the words settled his spirit, but nothing could calm the what-ifs in his mind.

Because if anything happened to Rachel or his little girl because of his choices, he'd never be able to forgive himself.

EIGHT

Rachel shut her office door at the company and leaned against it, letting her head drop back against the heavy wood. She had approximately five minutes alone to pull herself together before Marshall handled his small job with staff duty and she had to put her investigator face back on.

Maintaining her professional distance was proving to be more difficult by the minute.

She hadn't worked her way up from military police officer to investigator to team leader at Eagle Overwatch by letting her emotions run the show. This case was changing her, clutching her heart in a six-year-old's fist.

She braced her heels to keep from sliding to the floor into a puddle of mama-hearted tears. While she'd never been a mother, if this morning's drama was even a fraction of what parents felt on a daily basis, she wasn't sure she could handle the emotions.

Fear and fatigue had dogged her all night. There were moments when Rachel was convinced she could hear someone breathing. Sleep had arrived around sunrise, but only with the assurance that Thalia and Phillip were watching the house and the garage apartment.

She'd wrestled the PTSD monster in the past, and last night had brought back memories of mental and emotional battles she never wanted to fight again.

This morning had been worse. Watching Marshall and Emma say goodbye was the icing on a seriously bitter cake. While the little girl had been excited for the surprise trip with her grandfather and her new "friend" Thalia, the true reason for her departure made the forced cheerfulness of the adults even more morbid. Emma might not make it back in time for Christmas, not if they didn't get to the bottom of this theft ring quickly.

She was determined that Marshall would join his daughter at the safe house in the North Carolina mountains, even if they hadn't found anything by Christmas Eve. The thought of father and daughter separated for the holidays because of her failure to close this case was more than Rachel could carry.

Marshall had been silent on the drive to the company, barely acknowledging the gate guard as they'd pulled onto post. He was fighting the internal war that every soldier fought, the battle between family and duty.

She just wished she hadn't had to make the choice. Watching him suffer was about to do her in.

That didn't bode well for the state of their working relationship. If she was feeling this much, then she'd crossed a line and her personal life was interfering. She hadn't felt her heart engage this much since the early honeymoon days of her marriage to Robert.

It was time to downshift before she found herself drawn even more to a man she couldn't give her life to, not with her past and not if she was going to continue on in her job at Overwatch. While the army did its best to station husbands and wives together, there were few jobs at Camp McGee that would tempt a man like Marshall Slater. He'd resent her, turn on her.

He'd turn *away* from her.

Rachel nearly groaned, but she bit back the sound just in time. Marriage should never cross her mind. That path was filled with choking vines.

Footsteps echoed in the hallway. Rachel peeled her back from the door and straightened to her full height. The commanding cadence of that stride was unmistakable.

She checked the badge and pistol at her waist, then tugged at the hem of her navy blue sweater. With a bracing breath, she shouldered her backpack, pulled the door open and stepped into the hallway, waiting for him to round the corner. Her fake expression echoed the ones they'd all pasted on for Emma.

When Marshall appeared, he nearly undid the knot Rachel had tied around her emotions. Sure, they'd been around each other all morning, but his dark jeans and gray fleece jacket served to make him look stronger than usual. Somehow, the casual look coupled with his bearing spoke of authority that didn't need a uniform to back it up.

He looked up, as though he could feel her watching. Something like a flash of pleased surprise scraped away the melancholy, revealing the man beneath the soldier and the father.

Almost as quickly, he reverted to business mode. When he was a few feet away, he jerked his thumb over his shoulder. "I talked to staff duty. Told them we'll be around getting ready for leave. They won't make rounds for a while, so we should have the place to ourselves."

Rachel arched an eyebrow and clamped down on a smile. That had almost sounded like a teenager trying to make his case for a date.

Marshall must have heard the words as soon as they popped out of his mouth, because his eyes widened. "I just mean we shouldn't have to worry about any surprises."

Rachel laughed. She couldn't help it. After the tension of the morning, his slip tickled a tender place in her spirit that needed to feel joy. "It's all good." She chuckled as he bit back his own grin. "I get that you're not asking me out on a date." She turned and headed for the battalion building and the S-6 shop. "It's kind of nice to see you slip up."

"What exactly does that mean?" His footsteps dogged her heels, and amusement crackled at the edges of his words as they exited the building and crossed the small open area to the battalion. He held the door open for her, a relaxed grin lighting up his face.

At least he was breaking out of his funk. Maybe working today would give him a sense of momentum, a focus other than the time he was losing with his daughter and the danger that had forced their separation.

"You're one of the most squared-away commanders I've ever met." Rachel spoke over her shoulder as they approached the locked door to the S-6 shop. "I've worked with my share of excellent officers, but you seem to pride yourself on perfection. It's the thing that makes you tick. In the three months I've been here, I've seen a meticulous attention to detail that goes above the norm."

Behind her, Marshall didn't say anything, but his footsteps seemed to drag. When she unlocked the door, he leaned around her to see. "How do you have keys?"

"Eagle Overwatch has its ways." Ways she couldn't share with him. She pushed open the door and walked inside, scanning for threats.

He followed her into the room and cleared his throat. "I'm detail-oriented because there are too many opportunities to make mistakes. I've seen…" His words spoke to her own past mistakes and regrets.

"You've seen what?"

He shut the door behind them, plunging the room into a semidarkness lit only by a lone emergency light in the corner. He flipped the light switch and scanned the room as though what they were looking for might be sitting out in the open. Just as Rachel decided he wasn't going to answer, he looked at her. "I've seen a lot of tragic mistakes." He pocketed his keys, then slapped his hands together with a loud clap. "Okay, Captain, you're in charge. Let's rock and roll."

It took a second to follow his abrupt shift in demeanor, but Rachel decided to go with the new direction. They were here to search for clues, not to talk about their personal— or even their professional—lives.

She stepped up to the counter that divided the entry from the storage in the back. "First rule, if you see anything that rings alarms for you or that looks out of place, don't touch it. Don't even breathe on it. Call me and let me handle it." She hefted her backpack onto the counter. "Evidence collection has to be by the book."

"Roger that." Marshall pushed through the low swinging door at the end of the counter and stopped with his hands on his hips. "What are we looking for?"

"If I knew that, we'd all be home sipping hot chocolate." Sliding the backpack to the side, she rested her elbows on the counter and leaned forward. "We'll both do a cursory glance to look for anything out of place or different. I've placed a camera in here, but it was a quick job one evening, and I haven't gotten anything usable off it."

"Where?"

She pointed at the ceiling above Marshall's head. "That's not a smoke detector."

"Nice." He turned a slow circle. "Is it a three-sixty view?"

"No. One camera is aimed at the counter and one at the back of the room. There are big blind spots on both sides." She leaned farther forward on her toes, stretching tense calf muscles. "If we don't find anything useful, I'll install a better one before we leave."

He stopped his rotation when he faced her again. "What makes you so sure it's someone in the S-6?"

"I'm not sure, but it's where the evidence points. Those drives are the real thing. They're not clones written onto fresh drives. The serial numbers match machines that were supposed to be taken to the main recycle center, but they weren't. We initially looked at you because your drive was the first one found, and the thought was that you could have replaced it before you turned the machine in for life-cycle replacement. Now that we've intercepted drives from other laptops, you're cleared. Because all recycled machines come through S-6, the next easiest route is if someone here is switching drives or someone between here and the recycling center is making the switch."

"I'm guessing since they're all out of my company, you don't suspect anyone at the recycle center itself?"

"Yep. And it can't be a random person in the company, either. It would be exceptionally hard for someone to switch drives just by sneaking around and taking them out of random computers. You'd notice if you logged on one day and your hard drive had been exchanged with a new one."

"I'd hope so." Marshall scratched his cheek. "Even without someone coming after me personally, this is a lot to take in."

Yeah, he was a lot to take in.

Rachel winced. Yeah, *it* was.

"You okay?" Marshall strode to the opposite side of the counter from her. "You winced."

"My mind is spinning. Some work, some personal." That was a gross understatement if she'd ever made one. When he was close, the scent of his soap and the power of his presence overwhelmed rational thought.

"Personal?" He braced his hands against the counter in front of her and scanned her face. "It's hard for you, not going home for Christmas."

She shrugged, staring at his chest, but he slid one hand forward and laid it on hers, his fingers warm against her skin. "Don't lie. You know it was impossible for me to let Em leave. Unless we solve this, Christmas is going to be me and you."

Her gaze rose to his. Christmas with Marshall. It brought the same image that had sent her running at the food court. Family. Home. Right.

He swallowed so hard she could hear it, and his grip on her hand tightened gently. "So what if I was?"

"What if you were what?" Rachel's voice was low and breathless, the kind she and her college roommates had made fun of in romcoms, the kind she'd never heard come out of her mouth before.

"Earlier. What if I was asking you on a date?" His gaze was serious, as if a lot rested on the question. Then it dropped to her lips before slowly rising again.

The questions couldn't be ignored. Not the verbal one, and certainly not the silent request for her to tilt her head and meet him halfway.

Answering *no* would chill the air between them.

Answering *yes* would change both of their lives forever.

He wanted to kiss her.

The back of Marshall's mind yelled like an angry drill sergeant that this was the absolute wrong idea. That he was making promises he couldn't keep. That he couldn't protect her. That their jobs ensured they had no future together.

That there were bigger things to do right now than kiss the woman who had intrigued him like no other had in years. To kiss her the way he'd finally realized he'd been wanting to almost since the moment he'd met her.

But the drill sergeant couldn't compete with the woman standing in front of him. And his heart had already committed to answer her silent yes with action.

When Rachel turned her hand beneath his so that their palms met, it was all the response he needed. He closed the gap between them, meeting her in the middle as his hand slipped farther and their fingers curled together.

The kiss exploded in his head and drowned out the shouted warnings in his brain. It blasted away the impenetrable stone walls of excuses he'd built against her. The ones he'd built against every woman.

Rachel wasn't every woman. Something deep in his heart was thawing, and it was something that said she could somehow be his.

That he could somehow be hers. Gripping her hand tighter, he shifted and lifted his other hand to lay it against her cheek, deepening the connection between them.

This was right.

This was—

A door slammed, the heavy metal sound echoing through the building.

With a jerk, Rachel jumped away from him. She stood on the other side of the counter, fists balled at her sides and eyes wide. She pulled in deep breaths and looked around the room as though she'd landed on a strange planet and was trying to orient herself to new surroundings.

He could appreciate the confusion.

The sound of voices up the hall called a screeching halt to his emotions and kept that internal drill sergeant from screaming censure at him. He'd messed up, taken the lead in a way he never should have.

But that could all come later. Someone was in the building, and Marshall and Rachel were nowhere near where they were supposed to be.

Another door slam bounced up the hallway, and the voices stilled.

Rachel's hand went to her hip, where he knew she'd holstered her pistol. Before his eyes, she morphed from the woman he was falling for to the hardened investigator she had to be. "Is that staff duty?" Her whisper seemed loud in the quiet room.

"I don't know. He could be making rounds early." Marshall's heart was still beating with explosive force, but he'd lost the ability to discern if it was the woman in front of him or if it was adrenaline.

She grabbed her backpack and crept to the door as he slipped through the swinging one on the counter. Her head tilted as she listened. "They're not coming closer. We may be able to make it out of the building and back to my office without being seen. We'll have to move quickly." She drew her weapon and reached for the door handle without waiting for him to agree.

Then again, she didn't need his agreement. She was in charge.

Letting her take the lead when he felt more like stepping in front to stand between her and danger was one of the hardest things he'd ever done.

Rachel eased the door open and peeked into the hallway, then waved two fingers for him to follow.

He made sure the door was locked, then fell in close behind her as they crept silently up the hallway and eased out the door into the small courtyard. He followed her into the company building and up the hall toward her office.

Even though they were out of immediate danger of discovery, neither of them spoke.

Marshall felt off-kilter, like he was walking through the haze of a dream. It could have been the kiss. It could have been because he wasn't used to being protected by anyone, especially not the woman he was being forced to acknowledge had captured a corner of his heart.

A heart that warred with his head. This couldn't be right. He knew that Rachel was capable of taking care of herself and of him, if the need arose. But after he'd failed Maggie and lost her, his mind wouldn't stop punching at him that this was failure, too. That if they wound up in a shoot-out and Rachel died, it would be the second woman he'd allowed to die because of his mistakes.

When they reached Rachel's office, she slid the key into the lock and entered, holding the door for him and then easing it shut behind them.

In the deep darkness of the windowless room, Marshall didn't breathe until he heard the lock click.

"Stay still. I can't be sure no one followed us." Rachel's voice was nearly quiet, and a soft rustle indicated she was on the move. There was a soft click, and then the dim blue light of a computer screen chased away a small section of the darkness, revealing the shadow of her form as she stood at her desk. "Come here, but be careful."

Roger. She didn't want him banging into anything, and she didn't want to turn on the overhead light and let it spill out from under the door to indicate their presence. He waited for his eyes to adjust, then walked slowly around to stand beside her as she clicked through buttons on the keyboard.

The computer screen split into two windows, camera images from the S-6 shop they'd just vacated. One was aimed at the door and the counter, while the other was aimed at the back of the room.

Rachel was shoulder to shoulder with him. She turned her head and whispered, "It's probably staff duty, but just in case…"

Marshall forced himself not to notice how warm her breath was against his cheek and not to remember how warm her lips had been on his just a couple of minutes before.

He had to focus on the moment at hand. Rachel was watching that room for a reason. Just in case it was their bad guy, she wanted a front-row seat.

From the closed office in the back center of the building, they had no way of knowing what was happening next door at the battalion. They had no way of knowing if someone had spotted them and was sneaking up on them as they waited.

The hair on Marshall's arms stood up. This was like every bad horror movie ever filmed, the heroes waiting for the monster to sneak up in silence and attack. The dark corners of the room seemed to be filled with watching eyes and waiting weapons. He had to force himself not to breathe too fast.

He'd been in a firefight one night in Afghanistan, when the darkness was deep and the hiding places were too many. The same feeling from that awful darkness crept over him now. Wondering what was hidden from his sight. Wondering where the bad guys were. Wondering if there was already a bullet headed his way with his name on it. Trying desperately to focus on the mission instead of everything he had to lose.

Like Emma. Like Rachel.

"Look." She spit the word out abruptly, and her blue-shadowed finger pointed at the screen.

The door to the S-6 shop eased open, and a man slipped through back first, watching the hallway as he shut the door carefully.

No one should be in the building. No one should be in the S-6 shop.

They were about to find out which one of his soldiers was a traitor. Marshall held his breath as the man turned.

NINE

Marshall seemed to be holding his breath.

Rachel couldn't fault him. Her breath was stuck in her chest as well, an involuntary reaction to keep anyone from hearing her, even though it seemed the threat was in the building next door. Yes, it was irrational. There was no way the soldier knew they could see him.

This moment had the potential to be huge, to change everything and finally bring an end to her investigation and to Marshall's nightmare, but Rachel checked her expectations. It could simply be one of the men from the battalion who'd left behind a wallet or a cell phone.

As the man turned away from the door, a shot of recognition forced her to take a step back.

"Plyler." Marshall exhaled the name in a

fierce whisper that spoke of barely sheathed anger.

No doubt he was livid and hurt. Marshall had invited the soldier into his home for the holidays. Had listened to him talk about the hardships of his family back home on more than one occasion. And the man had repaid him by threatening his daughter? By attacking Rachel in an effort to inflict emotional pain?

Rachel reached for Marshall's wrist to keep him from bolting for the door, but he grabbed her hand and held on tightly, his tension adding extra strength to his grip.

Rachel ignored how right it felt to have his fingers laced through hers. Now was definitely not the time to be thinking anything emotional. She followed Sergeant Plyler's every move on the screen as he headed for the door in the counter, slipping a backpack from his shoulder as he went. "We need to wait for a minute longer. We don't know yet if he's here because he innocently left something behind or even if he's alone or not." There had been someone else in the hallway with Sergeant Plyler, but it was likely staff duty was merely checking on the soldier to see why he was in the building.

She hoped no one had alerted Plyler to their presence.

"Did you suspect him at all?" Marshall was still whispering, the moment too tense to speak any louder.

"I investigated him the same as everyone else in the battalion, but I haven't seen evidence that points to him." James Plyler worked in the S-6 shop, which had made her take a harder look at him, but there was nothing to make him stand out above any of the other soldiers who worked there. "He sets off zero alarms. No major purchases. No suspicious behavior."

On the monitor, Sergeant Plyler stood at the counter for a long moment, as though he was listening for something.

Rachel held her breath and only exhaled when he dropped his backpack on the counter and headed toward the back of the room, disappearing for an instant as he passed beneath the cameras. "What about you? Have you noticed anything?"

Marshall's shoulders moved, possibly a shrug. "He bought a truck not long before you got here, right after the battalion got back from overseas, but it was a used vehicle with no frills. Nothing fancy. And you can't point to a soldier fresh off a deployment buying a car as strange." He kept his voice as low as hers, although they could probably shout and not be heard.

A new car wasn't evidence. Plenty of soldiers socked away their hazardous duty and tax-free pay while they were gone. Big purchases were far from unusual. There were car dealerships that built their business models around returning soldiers.

No. The car wasn't enough. She needed more. She needed to catch him with the drives in his hand.

Plyler disappeared among the metal shelving toward the back of the room, out of sight of the camera's range.

Rising up on her tiptoes, Rachel fought the urge to rush into the other building with her weapon drawn and her handcuffs at the ready. This time, her fingers tightened around Marshall's.

She could not blow this. She had messed up in the past, but she couldn't now. The stakes were too high, and the lives involved were too important. "There's no back way out of S-6, right? No windows? No emergency doors?" There weren't any in her memory, but that didn't mean Plyler didn't have an escape route ready.

"No." Short. Clipped. Tense.

Just like she felt.

Minutes ticked by. Wild conjectures started to unfold in Rachel's mind and to edge her feet toward the door. Did he have a hidden tunnel? A secret door? Was there a wardrobe to Narnia right here in the battalion?

When Plyler finally came into view again on-screen, she and Marshall relaxed. She could almost feel the tension leaking from her feet into the ground.

"What's he holding?" Marshall lifted their joined hands and pointed at the screen.

Releasing his hand, Rachel leaned forward and zoomed in as much as she could without pixelating the image.

Plyler carried a stack of slim silver rectangles.

"Hard drives." Rachel was headed for the door before her words could even reach Marshall's ears. She had her man. "Call the MPs. And stay here."

He was close on her heels. "I'm coming with you."

"Not arguing with you." She hissed the words as she wrapped her fingers around the doorknob. "If this is not a by-the-book takedown, Sergeant Plyler could get off on a technicality." She hesitated before she pulled the door open, Marshall breathing down her neck. That was the biggest reason, but high on her radar was another, one she didn't want to acknowledge.

If he became injured or killed, she knew she'd carry that guilt for the rest of her life, not only because Emma would be an orphan, but because some small part of Rachel saw him as so much more than an asset to protect. "Just promise me you'll stay here."

"What if he's not alone? Who's got your back?"

There wasn't time to argue. She had to move. Now. If Plyler got out of the building, she might never have the chance to catch him almost literally red-handed again. "Stay. Here." Without turning back to see if he obeyed, she eased the door open and slipped out. As she slowly closed the door behind her, his low voice drifted back.

Good. He was on the phone with the MPs. She hoped he'd stay in the office after. She should only have to hold Plyler in place for a few minutes.

Slipping out of the company building and into the door of the battalion, she drew her weapon and prepared for whatever came next.

With her pistol held low, she crept up the hallway, keeping close to the wall, listening for doors or footsteps, but the building remained silent. If Plyler had a partner, perhaps the other man was waiting in an escape vehicle.

That was how she would have played it.

At the corner nearest the S-6 shop, she stopped and readied herself for action. She had to do this just right.

A click echoed in the hallway, then a soft scrape as the door to the S-6 shop swung open. Rachel held herself steady, waiting for it to close again so that Plyler couldn't duck back inside and barricade himself in to set up a standoff.

A dull thud as the door shut proved to be the sound she'd waited to hear for months.

Now or never.

Rounding the corner with her weapon raised, Rachel found herself looking at the backpack slung over Sergeant James Plyler's shoulder as he walked away from her up the hallway. He had the swagger of a man who thought he was once again safely getting away with his crimes. That backpack was everything, and she was about to take him down with it in his thieving hands. "Military investigator. Stop and lace your hands behind your head."

Plyler froze in midstep, then slowly lowered his foot. His hands remained at his sides.

"Hands behind your head. Now." From the building layout, Rachel knew no one could sneak up behind her, but there was always the possibility someone waited around the corner in front of her. Her eyes darted from Plyler to the unsecured area. She had to get him contained. "Lace your fingers behind your head and drop to your knees."

It seemed to take him forever to run through his options, but finally, Plyler lifted his hands slightly...

And let the backpack slide from his shoulder. It almost seemed to fall in slow motion. He bolted before the bag hit the floor, trying to flee without the evidence on him.

Rachel shouted and took off in pursuit. She could not lose Plyler, nor could she leave that backpack unattended. She snagged it as she passed, and Sergeant Plyler disappeared around the corner.

He could not get away. He just couldn't. But if he did, she had his fingerprints all over the drives and video on her laptop. That would be enough.

But it would necessitate a manhunt she wanted to avoid.

A loud crash echoed through the building,

and more shouts bounced against the concrete walls as the MPs ordered Plyler to halt.

Rachel dragged her feet to a stop and lowered her weapon, breathing heavily with tension and relief.

The thief was in custody, but her brain refused to feel relief.

Something wasn't right. As she watched one of the taller MPs handcuff Plyler, that nagging feeling grew stronger. Plyler was a wiry guy, thin and tightly muscled. The man who had attacked her had felt bigger somehow, bulkier and stronger.

Although her mind could be playing tricks on her, it was possible Plyler wasn't acting alone.

Marshall tugged on an old gray sweatshirt and pulled it down over the waist of his navy blue track pants. He kicked his towel across the bathroom's tile floor toward the plastic hamper. For now, his body was too tired to lean over and pick it up. A deep-down part of him wondered if he'd ever overcome the exhaustion that had sapped the last ounces of his strength.

He'd felt the same way in the first weeks after Maggie had died, when guilt and sorrow had warred with his need for rest. Back then, he'd been certain sleep would never win that battle. Eventually, rest had returned, though it had taken months.

He pulled open the bathroom door and let in the cooler, drier air of his bedroom. The change of air brought a change of memory, to another time when he'd begged for rest, but for a much different reason. Shortly after Emma was born, colic had wiped their house clean of any form of sleep for weeks. Eventually, things had leveled out. His daughter now slept like a champion.

Thanks to Rachel's apprehension of Sergeant Plyler, that same sweet girl was safely tucked into her own bed in her own house, free from any more threats on her life. She'd been disappointed that her holiday trip had been U-turned only an hour from their destination. In fact, she'd been vocal enough to earn a short time-out from her father. But ice cream for dessert and a promise to decorate the Christmas tree the next day had set everything right. The last time Marshall had checked on her, she'd been zonked out with a choke hold around her ever-present Dora the Explorer's stuffed neck.

His father-in-law had taken up residence in the guest room after deciding he didn't want to miss the festivities the next day. The man was a godsend, the extra eyes he'd needed on Em while everything descended into chaos. At nearly sixty, retired colonel Wes Brogden was as fit as he'd ever been. There was no doubt the man could take down any threat that came after his granddaughter.

But even Wes couldn't help with his current biggest concern.

No, according to a text from Staff Sergeant Thalia Renner, his current biggest concern was passed out from exhaustion at her own apartment. Although she'd overseen Plyler's arrest, Rachel still seemed restless and vigilant, though she wouldn't tell him why. The staff sergeant was enforcing the commander's directive that Rachel finally get some real rest.

Marshall swiped the condensation from his bathroom mirror and rested heavily on his palms as he leaned closer to his reflection.

All was well. The day was saved. His daughter was safe.

And he'd let Rachel do it all on her own.

She'd stood down Sergeant James Plyler on her own. Had pursued him on her own. Only the arrival of the MPs had stopped that pursuit from becoming a major altercation, Marshall was certain.

What had Marshall done? Dialed a phone

number and stood in her dark office, watching a computer screen. She'd ordered him to do it. He understood why.

But if anything had happened to her...

He'd battled the unwanted visions in his head all day, even as he'd welcomed his daughter safely back into their home. The images of Rachel bloodied, bruised or worse wouldn't stop. The imaginary pictures kept entwining with the real ones, the ones where he'd walked into his bedroom on post at Fort Carson to find Maggie gone.

His fault. All his fault.

There was no way he was going to be able to close his eyes tonight, not with imaginary nightmares and real ones running on a continuous loop.

Sometimes, he hated the guy in the mirror. He was a selfish human being. A man who stood down from a fight. A man who'd let his wife die.

Shoving away from the counter, he walked into the bedroom, the transition from cool bathroom tile to soft carpet warm under his bare feet. His bed was calling. He wished for no more surprise visitors. According to a brief earlier text from Rachel, Sergeant Plyler had confessed to being a one-man operation. There was no one left to sneak in.

Marshall had yet to unpack his feelings about a soldier he'd trusted and the man's treachery toward him and his daughter. Plyler had seemed like a nice kid, concerned about his family back home after a medical issue had forced his father into early retirement. There'd never been any indication that he could be violent.

But violence could hide in the open sometimes. That was one of the things that made this world so scary.

He really didn't want to think about it anymore. Marshall grabbed the remote from the nightstand and dropped onto the bed, but he popped back up again as soon as his head hit the pillow. Despite Rachel's assurance that Plyler had confessed to being a lone wolf, Marshall's alert system wouldn't shut down. Maybe it was because Rachel hadn't seemed to relax after Plyler's arrest. Being tucked away in his bedroom at the back corner of the downstairs felt hazardous somehow, as though he might miss something.

He tossed the remote to the bedspread and padded to the bedroom door. He could sleep on the couch. Then he'd know if someone tried to sneak in.

Marshall stopped with his fingers wrapped around the doorknob. The couch was no better. He'd slept on the couch the night Maggie had died, and look how that had ended.

All his fault.

The past few days had ripped the door off the vault where he held the memories of that night, and they roared in with a brand-new, hot kind of vengeance. He turned his face to the ceiling. "Are You ever going to stop punishing me?" He growled the question, although what he really wanted to do was unleash the inquiry with a roof-rattling roar.

God had some kind of business with him, and Marshall had no idea what it was. He wasn't even sure he wanted to know.

Grabbing his phone from the dresser, he shoved it in his pocket, jerked open the door and headed for the kitchen. There had better be soda in the fridge.

Grateful that his father-in-law and his daughter were tucked away upstairs, he flipped on every light in the living room on his way through, trying to chase the blood and the death into the darkness.

His hand was on the fridge door when the phone buzzed in his pocket, jolting his fingers from the fridge as though the device had shocked him. Plyler better still be in custody, and this had better not be bad news.

He glanced at the screen. Why are you up?

Rachel. Turning, he leaned back against the fridge and cradled the phone in his hands, staring at the screen before he typed. Why are you? Thought you had orders to rest, soldier.

I slept for a few hours.

Good. If she was anything like him, she could run on a few hours as long as they were solid hours. He'd eventually get some as well, but a caffeinated soft drink wasn't going to help matters. He moved to type again, then stopped.

Wait a second.

How did you know I was up?

Three dots appeared. Disappeared. Appeared again. Good guess?

Yeah, right. She was outside. The realization was a harder kick than caffeine could ever be. He opened the fridge, grabbed two cold soda cans, then stopped, gaze darting between the back door and the front of the house. Where would she be?

Rachel didn't play games. She wasn't flirting or being coy. She was here because she wanted to know all was well. In all likelihood, she couldn't sleep because she was as keyed up as he was, something in the back of her head not quite willing to believe everything was over and everyone was safe. It was the same kind of high alert that followed soldiers home from a war zone, the kind that led to restless roaming around on constant guard duty, even in the safety of their own homes.

She had to be sitting out front in her car, watching. He headed for the front door, shutting off all but one floor lamp as he crossed the living room. He twisted the dead bolt and pulled the door open.

Rachel stood on the porch in jeans and a fleece jacket, her hair up in that ever-present ponytail and wearing a sheepish expression on her face.

Marshall took one look, set the drinks on the table beside the door, pulled her to him...

And kissed her.

TEN

Swallowing a gasp, Rachel grabbed fistfuls of Marshall's sweatshirt and kissed him back. This wasn't why she was here. She'd come because her suspicions about Plyler not working alone had driven her to make sure everything really was okay.

But when he'd snapped on the lights, her feet had brought her to his door. She hadn't admitted why until she had what her heart wanted. Him close to her. His arms around her. Sheltering her. Accepting her. A kiss that said they could figure out a way to make this work.

Except they couldn't.

She had to be brutally honest about that.

Rachel jerked her head to the side and drew her lips between her teeth, trying to keep them from playing traitor. It took longer to convince her hands to release his sweatshirt, where his heart beat wildly against her fists.

Marshall dropped his arms from her waist when she let go. He backed away in slow motion, as reluctant as she was. The move left her on the porch and him in the house, the threshold of the door between them.

That seemed cruelly symbolic.

"I guess we should talk." His voice was hoarse and deep.

He had no idea how much they needed to talk. Rachel backed up to the top step and pointed to the street. "Can we walk? Thalia drove here. She can keep an eye on the house." Because she wasn't sold on Plyler's confession, not when she could still feel thickly muscled forearms trying to suffocate her.

Marshall arched one eyebrow. "Thalia's watching the house?"

Cheeks flaming, Rachel nodded. Thalia had seen her kiss Marshall. The other investigators in Overwatch still gave Trey Blackburn grief for falling in love with Macey Price while he was surveilling her, and the two of them had been married almost six months.

Rachel frowned. Trey and Macey were living a happy ending, but their situation was different. Macey was a civilian, a physical therapist who could do her job anywhere. Marshall and Rachel were soldiers whose jobs would never land them at the same post.

As though he could read her mind, Marshall's smile dipped. "I'll get my shoes. Want to come in?"

Yes, but no. If she did, she might never leave. She'd wind up wrapped in the embrace of his home and the warmth she desperately wanted for herself.

But she would never be enough for him. "I'll be on the sidewalk." She walked away, feeling his eyes on her back before the door eased shut.

Rachel faced the house, avoiding even a glance in Thalia's direction. The younger soldier would cheer on that kiss. But she had never been bruised by combat or divorce. Thalia had her own issues, but she'd never be able to understand Rachel's.

Marshall stepped onto the porch, locked the door and joined her on the sidewalk. He tilted his head to the left to direct their path as he shoved his hands into his coat pockets and started walking, stepping over tree roots that had broken through the sidewalk.

Tonight, she'd tell Marshall her story. There wasn't a choice if she wanted to stop this growing attraction. She fell in beside him, keeping distance so their elbows wouldn't brush. But there was other business to attend to first. "Sergeant Plyler is talking to the federal agents. He's laid out everything he did at the company."

"What about what he did to you and to me? Has he confessed to that?"

She kicked a crack in the sidewalk. She ought to tell Marshall her suspicions, but that was all they were…suspicions. There was no evidence to warrant scaring Marshall, not when her imagination could have made Plyler seem larger than life in the moment he was trying to kill her. She'd be vigilant. Marshall needed to rest. "Nothing yet. He's probably holding that close and hoping to bargain for a lesser sentence that doesn't involve attempted murder." She shoved her hands deeper into her pockets. "Is that what's keeping you awake?"

He chuckled, but the sound was as brittle as the chilled air. "That question isn't just loaded—it's a semiautomatic with a full clip."

"That bad?" She could spill her reasons why they wouldn't work later. Right now, something big was on Marshall's mind.

He sniffed. "I shouldn't have kissed you.

Not at the battalion and not just now. I'm sorry."

The words smacked as hard as any slap. She barely managed not to wince. Yes, she had to sever what was happening between them, but it stung that he'd swung the ax first.

Her pride bucked. "I was going to say the same thing."

"Well, at least we're in agreement." He trudged beside her, kicking a rock off the sidewalk into the street. "Miserably."

Rachel's nose stung deep inside where she stored tears she refused to shed. His acknowledgment that they both wanted what they couldn't have cut worse than the initial rejection. She knew her reasons. She could only guess his. "Is it because of Emma?"

He laughed softly. "Em babbled about you for days after you pushed her on the swings at that cookout. And she chattered all the way to school the other day about the fact that you were in our living room. She's a kindergartner and brutally honest. She didn't ask you to decorate our Christmas tree tomorrow just to be nice. She's fascinated by Captain Rachel."

"Way to twist the knife, Slater." Though their interactions had been brief, that sweet little girl had shone some light into the dark corners of Rachel's heart.

"Since we're being honest, I thought I'd be, well, honest." He elbowed her lightly in the bicep, then reset his distance. "We're both ripping off bandages here."

That was exactly what it felt like. A stinging tear beside an already-raw wound.

"It's not Em. Not exactly." Marshall's steps slowed, so Rachel cut her pace. Any slower and they'd be dragging their feet. "It's me. This past week has proved what I've known all along, and I can't bear to see you get hurt because of me."

His words echoed the cry of her own heart so loudly that he must be able to hear it. Rachel swallowed the words that wanted to pour out of her own story, but she needed to hear his first.

"Since I was your initial suspect, I'm sure you've read up on my history pretty thoroughly." Marshall grazed past a bush that had encroached on the sidewalk, his shoulder brushing hers. "You know Maggie took her own life."

Rachel drew her lips between her teeth and nodded. It was awkward to admit the background check had been so thorough that she could practically tell him how much money he'd spent on fast food last year.

"You probably don't know that my mother tried to kill herself when I was six, before she left my dad. I doubt that showed up in any paperwork."

Rachel's eyes slipped shut. How could Marshall have endured so much? "The divorce was there, but not the suicide attempt."

"I was at school the day it happened. I didn't know much about it until I was older. I just knew she left us and never came back. She's still alive—living in California, last I heard. I haven't seen her since I was eight."

So he'd been abandoned by someone he loved, too. Rachel's wounded heart tore over his pain.

He didn't notice. Instead, he seemed to be putting words together before he spoke again. "What no piece of paper is ever going to tell you is that Emma is not my biological daughter." He cleared his throat and tilted back his head. "And I essentially killed my wife."

Rachel stumbled and stopped in the middle of the sidewalk. What was he confessing? She was going to have to arrest the man, rip him away from his daughter. Why? "Marshall, be careful."

"I didn't murder her." He stopped and

faced her, but he didn't look her in the eye. Instead, his gaze was fixed over her, back the way they'd come, likely on his house. "But I wasn't there to stop her. She'd be alive today if I'd been there."

With a solid thump, Rachel's heart started beating again, but sweat clung to her skin underneath her jacket. She shoved up her sleeves and lowered the zipper a couple of inches, hoping the cold air would work quickly against her too-hot skin.

"We argued that night." He sniffed, glanced at her, then stared into the distance again. "We argued a lot. Maggie always struggled. She was struggling when I met her, and I guess I thought I could save her." He shook his head, lost in a moment from years before. "She was an amazing person. I loved her. But it wasn't enough."

His pain was too much. Maggie's death must have layered over his mother's own attempt and abandonment, wounding the man and the little boy inside. Despite her vow not to touch him, Rachel reached for his hand and laced her fingers through his.

He held on loosely, almost as though he was afraid of hurting her. He kept talking without making any other connection. "When I met Maggie, she had just come back from overseas. Was sent back, actually. She was having brutal panic attacks. I ran into her at a chapel service. She'd been…" He scanned the sky, the trees, the street, everything but Rachel. "She'd been raped on a forward operating base, but she never knew who did it. She said she was on guard duty, it was dark…"

Rachel gasped. She'd heard of such horrors, but she'd never personally known anyone who'd experienced them. She tightened her grip on Marshall's hand, trying to comfort Maggie through him. "She didn't report it." The military could be a fickle beast. Sometimes women were fortunate enough to be heard. Other times, in a male-dominated culture, ears and minds were closed.

"No. She told me once that a man had been harassing her, constantly asking her out. She suspected it was him, but…but she never moved forward. She'd seen too many complaints by other female soldiers dismissed in the past."

Sadly, she likely had, especially that many years ago.

Marshall exhaled loudly. "The day I met her, she'd just found out she was pregnant."

"Emma."

"That kid is the best thing that ever happened to me. Her birth certificate says she's my daughter, and no matter what DNA says, she is."

"I know." Anyone with eyes could tell that Emma was Marshall's world. He loved her with the kind of sacrificial love that would ensure that little girl grew up with confidence and grace.

"Maggie and I got to be friends. I was her sounding board. We spent a lot of time together, and we got closer. Or as close as Maggie could get to anyone. Her childhood was traumatic, like mine. Her mother wasn't in the picture, either. The PTSD from the incident ate away at her. We loved each other, and I wanted to protect her, so about three months before Emma was born, we got married. I guess I thought maybe then she'd feel safe." He inhaled deeply again, as though it took a lot of oxygen to get through his story. "She was fragile before Em was born, but she was severely postpartum after. Don't get me wrong—our good times were amazing. But our bad times?"

He worked his jaw back and forth. "She packed up Em and left me once. I wasn't capable of understanding what she was going through, and it led to a lot of arguments. One really bad night, I told her I'd had enough, that if she wanted to walk away she could, but she couldn't have Em. She screamed at me and threatened DNA testing. I walked out. Slept on the couch." His fingers tightened on Rachel's. "Well, I tried to sleep. Heard Maggie get up a time or two, almost went and apologized. Didn't. When I got up the next morning…"

His expression was so pained, Rachel couldn't stand to make him speak anymore. "It's okay. You don't have to tell me. I already know." She'd read the autopsy report. Maggie Slater had downed an entire ninety-day supply of clonazepam, a drug used to treat anxiety and aid with sleep, among other things.

"I still wake up sometimes seeing her in the bed that morning…" Marshall dropped her hand and turned toward the house. "It was my fault. I couldn't save her. I was too full of my own pride. And I won't let you suffer because of me."

There. He'd said it. For the first time in his life, he'd told someone everything. Some tiny part of him had hoped it would lighten the burden that weighed down his soul.

It didn't. Coming clean only made everything worse. As he'd talked, he'd sunk into Rachel's presence and the comfort she offered. It made walking away from her even harder than it had been before he spun his awful story. Marshall paced toward his house. There was no good ending to this mess he'd created.

"Marshall. Wait." She caught up to him in three steps, grabbing the back of his jacket. "Stop."

He obeyed, but he didn't turn around. He couldn't stand to see undeserved sympathy in her eyes. Couldn't stand to look at her at all, because it would only wreck his heart, a reminder of everything he'd lost that night. Not just his wife. Not just Emma's mother. But any future with anyone ever again. He was a terrible husband. A selfish one who couldn't understand his wife and who'd chosen to walk away from her when she'd needed him.

"Marshall, it's not your fault." Her grip tightened on his jacket and she stepped closer, her forearm resting against his back as she held on to him. "Your mother had bigger things going on than a child could handle. And Maggie had bigger things going on than even a grown soldier could ever handle."

"So do you."

At his words, she stiffened. Her breathing came heavier. She would let him go now, would back away and take off up the street and out of his life. He'd have to find a way to explain to Em that her new friend wouldn't be there tomorrow after all, but she understood that the army sometimes took people to places without explanation. She'd be disappointed, but—

"How did you know?" The words were a whisper.

"That was a panic attack you had at the food court. I recognized it." Maggie had had her fair share of them. There were days when he still wondered if she'd ever really trusted him.

"It was. But not because of anything in the food court. Not because of PTSD. Although I've battled it."

"And won?" Not that it mattered. She could always wind up in some other trouble that he couldn't save her from. He'd failed his mother. He'd failed Maggie. He had to channel all his energy into not failing his daughter. Because if he failed her, it would kill him. At times, he even considered walking away from his career to be there for her.

He couldn't add another person to his life, not when she might need what he couldn't give.

"I did. I mean, I struggle some days. I don't know that it ever really goes away." She was finally breathing normally again, her arm rising and falling in rhythm against his back. "It was rough for a while. I saw two good soldiers die in front of me. That doesn't leave you. So, yes, there were panic attacks. There was medication and therapy. There are still occasional bad days, and sometimes, there is therapy again. But it's not a death sentence."

"It was for Maggie. Emma wasn't enough to keep her here. I wasn't enough to keep her here." What had he just said? That thought, those words, had never even crossed his brain before. It wasn't just that he couldn't save Maggie, that he'd essentially walked away and let her die. It was that he hadn't been enough to live for.

"Maggie's decision had nothing to do with you." As though she could hear the ripping in his heart, Rachel rested her forehead against his back. "I don't know why some people let go of life. There are things I will never understand. That none of us will ever understand. And it hurts. I think we put too much on people who are struggling. If they had cancer or heart disease, we'd understand there are side effects and issues that we can't control. It's the same with mental illness, but we don't treat it that way. There are things we can't control, even when we're the ones struggling.

But instead of treating it like illness, we treat it like failure, either because we can't fix it ourselves or we can't fix someone else." She let go of his coat and slipped an arm around his waist. "And like cancer or heart disease, I don't know why some people find a cure and some people don't."

She didn't understand. No one ever could. He'd failed. Not Maggie. Him.

All her words jumbled in his head. Marshall pulled her hand from his waist and stepped out of her embrace, then turned toward her. "I failed her, but I refuse to fail you or Em. There's too much at stake, and I can't mess up again and drop the ball like I did the night that Maggie died. If I'd stayed with her, hadn't walked out on her, had slept in the same room with her..." He chopped the air between them with a flat hand when she stepped closer and tried to speak. "No. Em would still have a mother if I'd swallowed my pride that night. I'd still have a wife."

The way Rachel pulled her shoulders back and worked her jaw, she was about to argue with him all over again. But she wouldn't understand. She could never understand.

"Look." He backed one step away from her, half-afraid that if she reached for him again, he'd pull her to him and let himself forget for a couple of minutes that this would never work. "It's not worth talking about. You started this by telling me you had your own reasons for walking away from us."

That took some of the fire out of her fight. Her stance softened in the way of a soldier who'd just been released from battalion formation. She knew he was right.

Rachel shoved her hands into the pockets of her jacket. For a long time, she stared at the center of his chest, as though she might be rehearsing a spccch. Whatever she was about to say, it wouldn't be the full truth, not with the amount of time it was taking her to pull a story together.

He wouldn't argue with her, though. As much as he wanted to call her on whatever half-truth she was about to tell him, it would only be arguing in favor of what they both knew they couldn't have.

Finally, she flicked her gaze up to his before she started walking, stepping around him on the sidewalk, expecting him to follow.

Of course, he did.

"My reasons are pretty much all geography and career." She shrugged when he drew up beside her, and they continued their slow walk back to his house. "If you're climbing the ranks in the infantry, you'll move a lot.

I'm planning to spend my career working my way up through Eagle Overwatch. Even with the army's commitment to placing spouses together, there really isn't a place where our two careers will cross in order for that to happen." Her voice dropped lower, softer, as though she wasn't speaking as a soldier but as a woman who was about to say something she really didn't want to say and half hoped he wouldn't hear. "One day, you're going to want to be married again. You're going to want a mother for Emma. You deserve a wife who can live under the same roof with you. Emma deserves a mother who can be there to make her cookies and go to her softball games."

"Em's more of a soccer kind of girl." The air between them was too heavy. If he didn't inject some levity, they'd both wind up having to crawl home on their hands and knees from the weight of revelation.

She chuckled, but it was forced. "I'll be sure to get that right when I talk to her again."

They stopped in front of the house, and Marshall stepped around to look her in the face. "Look at us, talking like grown-ups." He could honestly say he'd never had a conversation like this with a woman. Open and honest, with all the emotions on the table instead of tap-dancing around feelings and possible embarrassment. Even with Maggie, though they'd been friends first, there had always been a veil between them, because Maggie had kept an emotional distance. After they were married, it had been hard to track her thoughts and feelings. She'd often talked to him about her struggles, but he always had the feeling she was holding back the worst to keep from hurting him.

Now here he was, holding nothing back, with a woman he could never call his own because of his mistakes, their careers and whatever it was she wasn't saying but that didn't matter in the long run.

"Speaking of Emma." She lifted her eyes and met his, holding the distance between them. She flicked a quick glance toward the car, where Thalia sat watching the house.

He knew she was thinking the other woman didn't need to witness any more public displays of affection, no matter how much Marshall wanted to kiss Rachel one last time. "What about her?"

"I promised to help decorate the tree with you all tomorrow. It may not be fair of me to just disappear."

"True. You and I are both grown-ups. We know where we stand. Emma has no expectations other than you being there to hang ornaments on the tree. You should be there." Not to mention he wasn't ready to tell her goodbye yet. No, they couldn't be together, but that didn't mean he couldn't tuck away a few memories to hold on to when she was gone.

"Far be it from me to wreck Christmas tree decorating day."

"Her father appreciates that."

She smiled and, with a small, awkward wave, turned and walked to the waiting sedan.

Marshall balled his fists in his pockets and dug his toes into the insoles of his boots. Every molecule in his body wanted to stride behind her and kiss her one last time, but he didn't. He couldn't.

Because if he did, he'd only fall further away from being able to tell her goodbye.

ELEVEN

Rachel licked green frosting off her thumb and watched Emma draw a lopsided yellow-icing star on a sugar cookie. Her morning with the Christmas tree had turned into an afternoon of baking refrigerated sugar cookie dough and decorating with store-bought icing. The sounds of a football game wafted in from the den, where Marshall watched with his father-in-law, munching the cookies Emma had delivered to them like the best of pint-size waitresses.

She should have told Marshall the truth. Keeping her promise to Emma today wasn't just about not disappointing a little girl. After her chat with Marshall, Rachel had reported her suspicions to her commander, who had agreed they needed to be investigated further. Until they could prove solidly that Plyler had been acting alone, the Slaters were still under guard. Thalia had stood watch last night. Rachel was staying close today.

She forced herself to smile past the pain the day was squeezing around her heart. Family Christmas activities dug at her chest, too much like what she'd always wanted for herself. She swallowed a wave of emotion that threatened to swamp her for good this time. "Great job on that one."

Shoving her braid over her shoulder, Emma frowned at her artwork from her perch on a step stool that had been shoved up to the counter so that the little girl could better reach the cookies. "It's uneven."

"All stars are uneven. In fact…" Rachel set her tube of green icing to the side and held her hand out for Emma's yellow icing. When the little girl dropped the tube into her palm, Rachel rotated it and smeared a huge round blob of yellow icing onto the cookie closest to her. "That's what stars really look like."

Emma giggled, the carefree sound prying another nail out of the fence Rachel was desperately trying to build around her heart. "You're right, Captain Rachel. When Daddy and I sit in the deck chairs and look at them, they look like that. Except white and not yellow."

Captain Rachel. An army brat all the way,

Emma had latched on to Rachel's rank and insisted on calling her that instead of "Miss." But Emma had also declared that, since she was not in the army like her daddy was, she got to use Rachel's first name. Captain Rachel she'd been christened by the tiny general who clearly ran the world.

Emma leaned closer, her shoulder pressing into Rachel's arm, and whispered, "So one time, Daddy took me outside to see a bunch of shooting stars, but he didn't know the back door was locked." She giggled again. "We slept in the truck because we couldn't get back in until the neighbors who had our key got up."

Rachel laughed despite her concerns. "Is that true?"

"Uh-huh. We were going to sleep on the deck, but it started to rain. And Daddy said he was glad he bought a truck with buttons on the door, or else we'd have had to sleep under the slide on the swings." Emma collapsed into laughter that draped her over the counter and brought Rachel's own low chuckle out to play.

"Are you laughing at my 'world's greatest dad' moment?" From the doorway to the kitchen, Marshall's voice washed deep over their laughter, sending Emma into even louder fits of hilarity.

His presence chopped off Rachel's joy at the root. Marshall had largely kept his distance all day, either staying on the opposite side of the room or, like this afternoon, hanging out in the other room while she spent time with Emma. But she hadn't missed that he was on his third soda since lunch. Either he kept coming into the kitchen because of her, or he was immensely stressed by her presence in his house.

Right now, his smiling eyes were locked on her instead of on his daughter.

Rachel purposely turned away and started capping the tubes of frosting. The longer she stayed, the harder it was going to be to leave.

It was already going to be like leaving half of her heart behind.

Emma cued in immediately. "Are we finished? There's still three more cookies left to decorate."

"Yeah, Captain Rachel." Marshall's voice held a teasing tone that sent warm shivers up Rachel's arms. "You can't leave three cookies undecorated. That's just un-Christmassy."

"I'm leaving those three for your daddy." He was too much. She couldn't do this tug-of-war with herself any longer. Sooner or later, she'd lose. It would be so easy to pretend that they could have everything, but when reality set in, the goodbyes would rip them all to shreds. As much as she didn't want to hurt herself or Marshall, she definitely didn't want to cause that kind of pain for Emma.

She should pull him aside, tell him why she was really here, then watch from a distance, the way Thalia and Phillip did. There was really no reason for her to interact with the family, not while they were safely at home.

"Those three cookies will have to wait." Marshall walked over and scooped Emma into his arms. He draped her upside down over his shoulder, launching a waterfall of hysterical laughter. "We have to get ready to go to the Christmas light show tonight, little girl."

Rachel's head jerked back. They were going to do what?

"Christmas lights!" Emma's shriek could break glass.

Pulling her around under his arm, Marshall rested her on his hip and placed his forehead to hers. "Okay, little bit." For the moment, Marshall only had eyes for his daughter. "Run upstairs, wash off the icing on your hands and pick out what you want to wear tonight. Something warm. But don't put it on until after we eat a little something, okay?" At her nod, he started to settle her onto the floor, but then he spun toward Rachel. "And tell Captain Rachel goodbye, because she'll probably have to leave before you come back down."

Emma practically leaped into Rachel's arms, rocking her a step backward. The little girl wrapped her arms around Rachel's neck and her legs around her torso, squeezing with all her might. "'Bye, Captain Rachel."

Her professional thoughts crumbled. Rachel hadn't been hugged with the innocence of a child since she left her job as a nanny when she graduated from college and moved on to full-time service. It had nearly ripped her in two that last day, saying goodbye to Braylen and Riley. Hugging Emma brought back that pain and stacked some more on top of it.

With a smacking kiss on Rachel's cheek, Emma wriggled free and ran for the den, hollering a hello to her grandfather as she went.

Her rambunctious departure left Rachel feeling empty-armed and frozen.

Marshall watched Em with a grin, then turned to Rachel and tilted his head toward the back door, the one leading to the deck where this whole thing had started. "Walk you out?"

No, he couldn't. There was no way she could leave him without telling him he was still under protection, that she had suspicions about his safety that made leaving the house a very bad idea. "I don't think—" Her phone vibrated in her hip pocket.

Seriously? Holding up one finger, she pulled the cell out, then answered. "Thalia. Shouldn't you be sleeping?"

"Are you still at the Slater house?"

Rachel reached out and braced her hand on the counter. Bad news was coming. There was no doubt. "Why? Has Plyler confessed to more?" *Ratted out his accomplice?*

Beside her, Marshall froze. Tension radiated off him, causing her own muscles to tighten.

"He hasn't confessed any more than we suspected initially. I just talked to Phillip, and he's still singing away to the guys who've been questioning him. He's been doing exactly what you suspected, sending dummy drives to be destroyed and selling the real ones. But he still swears he never came near the Slater home or vehicle and that he's been working alone."

Rachel drew her eyebrows together as

Marshall stepped closer. She cast him a quick, worried glance. "But what about what I was thinking?"

"That's the thing. You were right."

Rachel shouldn't have eaten those three cookies earlier. They coagulated in her stomach under the weight of Thalia's words. "How do you know?"

"Plyler gave us permission to test his DNA against the sample from your fingernails, and we just got the results back. The DNA from your fingernails doesn't match his. You were right. Plyler didn't attack you. Someone else did. This isn't over. Marshall and Emma Slater are still squarely in danger."

This might be the stupidest thing he had ever done. Rachel had already repeatedly told him so.

Marshall gripped the steering wheel and followed Thalia's sedan as she threaded through parking lot rows, searching for three spaces together at McGregor Park for Christmas on the Cumberland. In his rearview, Staff Sergeant Phillip Campbell's headlights reflected. He was hemmed in before and behind by bodyguards.

Bodyguards who had crawled under his

vehicle earlier to make sure no one had managed to tamper with it in his garage.

All so his daughter could go to a light show.

In the back, Emma rested safely in her car seat beside her grandfather, and they had kept up a rousing round of Christmas carols since leaving the house. Rachel rode in the front seat, answering Emma with a humor that seemed real when she was addressed, but that was likely fake. From a distance, the vehicle was the picture of Christmas cheer.

Except for the driver's seat. Marshall had navigated the drive to the river walk in silence, constantly watching traffic for the vehicle that might come at him.

Worse, every time he glanced to the side, he noticed Rachel's surveillance. Although she seemed to be fully engaged with Emma, her gaze never stopped scanning the windows.

The only place she never looked was at him. Her disapproval at this outing screamed louder with every second she refused to look directly at him.

When Rachel had hung up the phone with Thalia, she'd led him out the back door and onto the deck, admitting that the man who'd attacked her was still at large. They were still waiting for access to the DNA database to do a broader search, but they were certain it wasn't Plyler.

They'd gone back and forth over this outing. Rachel wanted to send the family to the North Carolina safe house again. She had Thalia on standby to travel while she stayed behind to investigate.

But he couldn't do it. Em had already been dragged halfway to North Carolina and back once. It was only two days until Christmas Eve. She needed stability. If he sent her away, there was no telling what that kind of uncertainty would do to her. He had no desire to restart the night terrors that had plagued her after Maggie's death.

He'd filled in his father-in-law on the situation, and they'd decided to keep Emma's world as steady as possible. With three Eagle Overwatch investigators, a retired army ranger and Marshall in their party, it was possible they were safer in public than they were at home.

He eased into a parking space and shifted into Park.

The back seat erupted into cheers, overly loud and manufactured by his father-in-law to distract Em.

Rachel finally looked at him. "You know you're in denial, right?"

The words were quiet enough to remain between them, but they carried the weight of her anger. Maybe she was right, but his daughter deserved some stability and not another broken promise.

Rachel watched him, her blue eyes shadowed. The darkness did little to hide her concern.

Marshall moved to speak, but little arms wrapped around his neck from behind and pulled him backward. "Daddy!" Emma shrieked in his ear.

Coughing, Marshall untangled her arms from around his windpipe. He didn't need to worry about an assassin. His daughter's exuberance might do the trick.

He needed to get his head into this game before Em picked up on his fear. She'd been looking forward to their trip to the light show since last year's visit. Despite the danger, this was the right thing to do for her.

Pivoting, he grabbed his daughter under the shoulders and hauled her over the console into the front seat.

Her kicking foot narrowly missed Rachel's injured cheek.

At least Rachel smiled.

Settling Emma onto his lap, Marshall pulled her to his chest. Part of him wanted to bundle her into the car seat and flee into the night.

But then she wiggled and poked his ribs, trying to tickle him beneath his heavy coat. "Daddy, we have to go. We need hot chocolate. And a cookie. And to see the lights."

"Yes, we do, kiddo. Every single one of them." He scrubbed his two-day beard against her soft cheek, eliciting another round of excited giggles and another barrage of kicking feet for Rachel to dodge.

He'd better stop before Em took down the person working to protect them.

"Okay, that's enough." He pulled her upright and shoved the door open as he glanced out the windshield.

Thalia waited in front of the vehicle. No doubt Phillip was behind.

That dampened the Christmas spirit.

Rachel opened her door, but before she could exit, Em scrambled out of Marshall's arms and onto Rachel's lap. "Captain Rachel's walking with me."

Rachel froze, but then she cleared her throat. "Sounds like fun."

Given last night's conversation, today could not have been easy for her. It definitely hadn't been easy for him. He'd been acutely aware of her presence. From decorating the tree to icing cookies, she'd seemed to fit.

But she couldn't, so he'd forced himself to stay planted in his recliner, keeping her out of sight.

He'd also downed an exceptional amount of caffeine. Rachel and her team could protect him from an assassin, but they couldn't stand between him and a heart attack if he didn't lay off the soft drinks.

Emma lunged for the door, but Rachel kept a tight hold as they piled out of the truck.

Marshall watched them before he slid out of the vehicle. Given the situation, Em was probably safer under Rachel's care than his.

With Thalia in front of the group and Phillip behind, they headed for the festivities. Before them, Christmas lights spread along the sidewalk that wound beside the river. The water reflected a distorted image of the colors, as murky and unclear as Marshall's thoughts.

Emma, one hand safely clasped in Rachel's and the other in her grandfather's, chattered as they walked behind Thalia. Phillip walked with Marshall.

It would take a tank to get to his little girl.

Marshall pulled in a deep breath and relaxed, drawing a sympathetic glance from Phillip.

"She's safe, sir. We'll make sure of it."

"Thanks." Hearing someone else say it almost made it feel true.

"I have a younger sister. I'd throw myself in front of a bullet for her. I can only imagine what you feel like with your kid."

"I hope you never have to find out."

Phillip nodded, his attention focused on the people around them as the crowd thickened.

Emma stopped and peered over her shoulder to search for him. "Daddy, hurry up!" She released her grandfather's hand to reach for him.

So she did remember he was there, even though she was enthralled with Captain Rachel. Marshall slipped in as Wes slowed to take up a position beside Phillip. Emma walked between him and Rachel, swinging their arms as she chattered about hot chocolate and lights and snow.

His heart whispered, but he definitely heard it. This was one of those right moments in life—Emma walking along between him and Rachel.

He ought to put a stop to this, either pick up Em and carry her or step back and let her walk alone with Rachel, but this was too warm and perfect, even if it was temporary.

And an illusion. He ought to be watching for threats.

He eyed the crowd and refused to look at Rachel. If they locked eyes, he might forget everything he knew to be true. Like the fact that, someday, he'd wreck her life. His pride and selfishness would destroy her as surely as they had destroyed Maggie.

But what if he was wrong? Rachel's words from the night before had chased sleep away. Would he blame himself if Maggie had died of a physical illness? He exhaled loudly. If only the December chill could clear out his thoughts the way it cleared out his lungs.

Emma stopped walking. "What's wrong? This is supposed to be fun!"

She was picking up on his unease and the rest of the party's vigilance. Marshall turned his focus to his daughter. "This is the most fun night of the year so far, right?"

"Right." Emma's pigtails bobbed with her nodding head.

"Let's get tacos from the food truck. On me." For Em, he'd pretend that everything was normal.

Up ahead, a long walkway arched by brilliant Christmas lights waited to admit them to wonderland. Marshall reached for his wallet to make good on his taco promise.

His back pocket was empty. Seriously? He'd stashed his wallet in the cup holder between the seats, in plain view of anyone who happened to peek into his windows. He stepped off the sidewalk out of the flow of traffic, and the rest of the group gathered around him. Only Phillip and Thalia stood apart, watching people pass.

Wes's eyebrows drew together over green eyes that looked exactly like Maggie's. "What's the matter?" He glanced around to see what had agitated Marshall.

"Wallet's in the car." That was embarrassing to admit, considering he'd just offered to treat everyone. "I'll run back and get it. Y'all go ahead and get in line."

He'd turned to walk away when Rachel grabbed his arm. "Leave it. You're not running around alone."

"As long as it's out of sight, it will be fine." Wes was already reaching for his own wallet. "I'll take care of the food."

"It's not out of sight, though." The last thing he needed was for someone to take advantage of his absentmindedness by wiping out his bank account. He turned to Rachel. "Let everyone else stay with Em. You and I can get there and back quickly. It won't take but a second."

He expected her to argue, but she simply nodded, then turned to Phillip and Thalia, who had flanked his family and were watching the crowds on the sidewalk. "You guys keep an eye on everyone else. Marshall and I will run to the truck and catch up with you in a minute. It won't take long."

Thalia pinned Rachel with a look that said she didn't think splitting up was wise, but Rachel's direct gaze prevented her subordinate from arguing. He got the feeling that this team often spoke more freely than they did in the regular army, but that protocol was still enforced.

He also got the feeling that Rachel was in no mood to be crossed tonight. "I have my radio if we need anything." She gave her teammates a curt nod, then turned and urged Marshall to walk alongside her.

They headed to the parking lot with hurried steps. Rachel never spoke, simply kept her head moving from side to side, making contact with every passerby and watching every shadow.

As they approached the SUV, he clicked the button, and the lights flickered. He'd get in and out quickly, so that they could get back to Emma and to Rachel's team. Maybe then they'd both relax a bit.

In the narrow space between his SUV and another almost exactly like it, he squeezed between the door and the driver's seat, reaching in to grab his wallet as Rachel stood near the rear of the vehicle, silently keeping watch.

He wanted so badly to say something to her, but he had no idea what the words should be. They couldn't have what both of them wanted, so there was no need to talk it to death. He'd enjoy her presence while he could and grieve what he'd lost after she had moved on.

Leaning into the SUV, he grabbed his wallet and moved to straighten.

Motion to his left, at the front of the car, turned his head as a man rushed forward from the darkness and slammed into the driver's-side door, ripping pain through Marshall's legs as he pitched into the vehicle.

TWELVE

The car rocked as a thud sounded behind her. Marshall half shouted a wounded cry.

Rachel reached for her weapon and whirled toward the front of the vehicle. What had just happened?

Marshall was slumped over the driver's seat, struggling to shove the door off him and to stand. He grimaced in pain when his eyes met hers. "Rach..."

Motion on the other side of the door dragged her attention away from him. A man wearing a ski mask and a forest green hooded sweatshirt backed away from the driver's-side door.

Plyler's accomplice.

Whatever happened next, this was going to end now. Rachel raised her weapon and took aim, her pulse hammering. With her left hand, she reached for her phone.

Through the window, the man's dark eyes locked onto Rachel's, the corners wrinkling as his mouth turned up with a chilling smile. "I wouldn't touch that phone. Not if you don't want me to shoot him through the door." The fake Aussie accent grated her nerves.

Rachel hesitated. She couldn't see a weapon, but then again, she couldn't see his hands, either.

His smile widened. He knew she couldn't get to him without leaving Marshall to round the vehicle. He was also bound to know she wouldn't pull the trigger on him here, not with Marshall between them and the occasional passerby walking on the greenway several feet behind him. The narrow space between the two oversize SUVs prevented anyone passing by from seeing what was happening.

She could shout for help, but there were too many variables. If this guy bolted and grabbed an innocent civilian or, worse, a child to ensure his getaway…

Rachel swallowed a small jolt of fear and leveled her weapon. If enough time passed, Thalia and Phillip would assume something was wrong and would hurry over to back her up.

This man probably knew that, too.

It might be a thin hope, but it was all she

had. "Back away from the door. Raise your hands where I can see them."

"Interesting how you keep showing up, Lieutenant." The man spit her rank, then glanced down at Marshall, who'd finally come to his feet but was wise enough not to get into her line of fire. Rachel gave him a quick once-over. It was clear he was injured, but she couldn't tell how badly without taking her focus off his assailant.

Marshall turned slowly and leaned against the driver's seat, warily eyeing the man who was watching him. Deep lines etched around his eyes and mouth, tinged white with tension and pain. "What do you want from me?" His words were forceful, but it was obvious the effort of speaking them came at a cost.

While the attacker's attention was on Marshall, Rachel edged a step closer. She was so close to success. Too close. But Marshall and the door between them might as well have been a thousand miles. She couldn't fire. Couldn't grab the guy. Couldn't shout loud enough to bring Thalia or Phillip on the run. She was on her own.

There was no way to win.

The man flicked an unconcerned glance at Rachel, then turned to Marshall. His lip curled into a sneer. "Captain, you stole my life. I'll have it back before this is over, but not until you've suffered like I have." With a violent shove, he slammed the car door onto Marshall's legs.

Marshall cried out and bent double, grabbing his shins where the door had cracked into them.

The man ran around the vehicle, angling toward the street and away from the crowds at the river walk.

Rachel turned to give chase but stopped. She couldn't leave Marshall unattended, not if this was a bluff. Holstering her weapon, she dropped to her knees beside Marshall and grabbed her cell phone, dialing Thalia's number. "Protect the family. We've had an incident." She reached for Marshall, and he grasped her forearm, letting her help him up to sit on the seat.

He leaned heavily against her, his weight nearly taking her down.

"Status?" Thalia's voice was deadly serious.

"Stay away from the vehicle until I give you the all clear. Suspect on foot, headed north toward Riverside Drive, away from your location. You're probably safer in the crowd." She hoped. "But be ready to move within the next two minutes." She wanted to be sure the man didn't circle back.

"How's Marshall?"

Rachel glanced at him. "Stand by." She knelt and eased his jeans up above his shins, wincing as he groaned. Angry red marks were already bruising, a double row of them standing out on his shins. Brow furrowing, she laid one hand against the back of his calf and felt his shins for breaks, wincing when he groaned at her touch. "How bad does it hurt?"

"I doubt he broke anything, but he came close." Marshall breathed the words through a clenched jaw. Rachel had whacked her shin on a car door enough times to know it hurt. Being slammed with one twice with the full force of a grown man behind the push had to be a wildfire kind of pain.

"We're going to get everyone out of here. Then I'm having Thalia transport you to the ER to get X-rays just in case." As much as she wanted to be the one to take him, she knew Marshall wouldn't go unless Rachel remained at the house with Emma.

"No." He closed his eyes and breathed deeply several times. "Just give me a second."

It was going to take a whole lot longer than

a second for the amount of pain he was bound to be feeling to pass, but Rachel turned her back to him, scanning the street and the parking lot. If Marshall's assailant was smart, he was long gone. The probability was high that they were all safe from him for the next few minutes, but she couldn't stop her skin from crawling.

She also couldn't stop her mind from screaming that she'd once again missed it. She'd let Marshall talk her out of protocol and into this public jaunt when they knew Plyler wasn't acting alone. She'd been armed and had the bad guy in her sights, and she still hadn't been able to keep Marshall from getting hurt. She hadn't been able to put a halt to the danger stalking him and Emma.

"Update?" Thalia's voice came through the static.

Rachel had forgotten she was on the line. "Hurt, but not badly." She held the phone close to her mouth and tried not to talk loudly enough for Marshall to hear, although since he was only a couple of inches behind her, that was essentially impossible. "I think our guy's gone, but get back here. Don't alarm Emma or her grandfather, but this outing is over." While Marshall was insistent on stability for Emma, he had to accept that this was foolish. Rachel couldn't let emotions play into her decisions again.

"Be there ASAP."

Pocketing her phone, Rachel glanced at her watch. Hopefully, Marshall would have time to recover enough not to scare Emma when she returned.

Marshall had slid back onto the driver's seat and was sitting with his elbows on his knees, his hands clasped so tightly that his knuckles were white.

She laid her hand on top of his. "Don't tense up. It makes the pain worse." The advice might seem counterintuitive, but it was true.

His brow furrowed, but then he visibly tried to relax. "He said I stole his life. What does that mean?"

"Is there anyone you've ever come down hard on? Been responsible for a demotion or having someone chaptered out of the army?"

"I mean, yeah, but anyone in command has had a hand in that at some point." He winced. "And that's not stealing a life. Taking it. I don't know."

Rachel leaned against the side of the vehicle beside where he sat, still surveilling the area. A new idea was forming, one that almost made her sick with dread. "I don't think these attacks are about the hard drives, not given what he just said about his life and the fact he didn't outright kill you. If he wants revenge and to make you pay, not to kill you outright, this is deeply personal for him."

"But what?"

Rachel shook her head. The suspicion was too twisted, too terrifying to air until she had proof.

Because the attacks might not have anything to do with Marshall.

And everything to do with Emma.

"So what's the plan?" Thalia poured a cup of coffee from the pot on the kitchenette's counter, then turned and leaned against it as she sipped the brew straight.

Rachel winced from her spot on the couch. That had to burn.

From where he sat at the window watching the house, Phillip matched her expression, though he said nothing. He looked as tired and defeated as Rachel felt.

Both of her junior team members had been unusually silent since they'd arrived back at Marshall's house. Phillip and Thalia had made a security sweep through the house and yard while Rachel helped Marshall inside as much as he'd let her. Walking had to be painful and would likely be worse tomorrow, but he'd managed to make it to his recliner without Emma suspecting anything other than Daddy didn't feel well and had to come home. A promise of more cookies and a favorite bedtime story with her grandfather had dried up tears and headed off a public tantrum.

If only it were that easy to settle grown-up emotions. Rachel's were all over the place, from relief to guilt to a slimy dread. "Right now, I'm battling hard-core déjà vu." Rachel scrubbed her hands against her cheeks. They'd just been right here in Marshall's garage apartment talking about plans, hadn't they? She'd caught the bad guy just yesterday, right? Why couldn't this be over? "Maybe I'm finally asleep and this is a giant nightmare."

"Nope. We're here again." Thalia swigged her coffee. "Here and waiting on you for answers, *boss*." Her tone bit off at the end, something edging the words with a bitter aftertaste.

Rachel sat straighter. "Do you have something you need to say to me?" Everything else was falling apart. Why shouldn't her team fracture, too?

Phillip turned from the window and looked

between the two women, his expression making it clear he'd rather be anywhere but here. "I think I'll head over and have that talk with Marshall about going to the safe house, if that sounds good." Without waiting for Rachel's agreement, her junior investigator headed out the door, closing it softly behind him.

As soon as his footsteps descended down the stairs, Rachel stood and faced Thalia head-on. The younger woman tended to pop off at the mouth on occasion, to speak before she thought. It was one of the reasons she hadn't been given more responsibility on a team yet. Still, she was typically friendly and easygoing. While her mouth was an issue, the disrespect was new.

"Only if I can speak freely." Thalia settled her coffee cup on the counter and stood tall, planting her hands on her hips.

"I don't have time for games." Rachel rolled her eyes toward the ceiling and counted to ten. She threw in a quick prayer that she'd be able to hold her temper and to speak whatever it was that Thalia needed to hear. "When have we ever stood on formality on this team? You know you can say whatever you need to say."

Tapping her index finger against her hip, Thalia regarded Rachel as she chewed her lower lip. Finally, she sighed, and her posture seemed to lose some of its starch. "You blew it back there." The words were matter-of-fact, maybe even sympathetic, lacking the acidity that had laced her earlier comment.

"I know." Rachel had been beating herself up for the past hour with all the things that could have gone worse and all the things she should have done. She should have insisted Marshall leave the wallet where it was. Should have kept the group together. Should have been watching Marshall instead of the parking lot.

Should never have let her feelings for a man and his daughter override the need for safety.

"You could have gotten yourself killed." Thalia's words fell hard against Rachel's soul. She'd considered the danger to Marshall, but she hadn't let it drift closer to home. "That's twice on this investigation. In less than seventy-two hours."

"I get it. Thanks." Stalking to the window, Rachel jerked the tie from her ponytail and redid the entire thing. Something about the motion made her feel more put together and in control. If only the rest of the situation was that easy to fix.

"Look, some things are pretty clear." Thalia

walked over and pulled a chair away from the table, settling next to Rachel's spot at the window. "You have feelings for Captain Slater."

There was no point in arguing. Thalia had had a front-row seat to their kiss the night before. She'd teased her about Marshall almost from the moment Sergeant Plyler had been handcuffed. There was no rolling back what she'd allowed Thalia to not only witness but to poke at her about. Rachel knew how to admit when she was wrong. "Every bit of this is unprofessional."

Thalia leaned closer and looked up at her, her chin practically hitting Rachel in the bicep. "You know, it was one thing when the investigation was wrapped up in a bow. When Plyler was the only threat and everything was over. It was kind of..." She bobbed her head back and forth, dark ponytail swinging. "...cute, you and the captain."

"Cute?" Rachel spit the word. "Nothing about any of this is cute." Even if the investigation was finished, there was no way to safely navigate their pasts or their futures. She walked away from Thalia and stood in the living area, staring at the bed where she'd nearly died. "None of this is cute. It's dangerous."

"Yes, it is. And you knew that the instant

that DNA came back without a match to Plyler. We all did." Thalia's voice was tinged with blue regret. "Captain…"

Rachel winced. Thalia almost never called her by her rank. She was drawing a line that Rachel should have drawn herself, the one between her heart and mind, between woman and investigator. The line she'd crossed with Marshall. "I know. I need to walk away."

"Can you?"

That was the problem, wasn't it? "Phillip and you are perfectly capable of protecting the Slaters. So is any other team in our unit." But this was bigger than protection, and it was time to tell her suspicions. Suspicions she'd be forced to investigate from a distance while Phillip and Thalia stayed on-site. "Thalia, there's more. And I want to keep this between me and you until we have hard evidence, but I think I know what this is about."

"It's not about Plyler?"

"No." Rachel wrestled the nausea in her stomach. She was about to reveal Marshall's secret, but she had no other choice. "Maggie Slater was raped overseas before she met Marshall. Less than a year before Emma was born."

"Okay. You think this has something—"

Thalia's eyes widened. "No." She pressed a hand to her mouth and walked to the door, staring at the drawn curtain over the window. "No. You think whoever raped Maggie is after Emma?"

"I hope not, but based on what our bad guy said to Marshall tonight, this is intensely personal. And few things are more personal than a man's children."

"You realize this is a huge stretch. We could simply be dealing with a serious sociopath here."

"Or a man who was obsessed with Maggie Slater and only recently found out his violence led to Maggie having a child."

"A child that Marshall is raising." Thalia came back and crossed her arms. "But where do we start? I mean, we have the DNA from your fingernails, but nothing will happen with that until we get blanket access to the database. That could take a while. Given the slowdown for the holidays, the court could take days to weeks to give us what we need to run that DNA against the system. If we could give a valid reason for narrowing the search down to a certain group, that would help."

"Let's start with Maggie. I'll dig into the men who were on her forward operating base. We can cross-reference those names with men currently in the company and see if any cross over, although we'd need more evidence than a coincidental deployment." Wait. *Currently in the company.*

"Thalia." Rachel whirled and faced her teammate. "Why didn't I see it before?"

"What?"

Holding up a hand while she processed the thought, Rachel pulled her phone from her hip pocket and called Alex "Rich" Richardson, their acting commander since the major had left to go skiing with his family.

Rich answered on the second ring. "Richardson."

"I think I know how to take down whoever is after Captain Slater." Before Rich could ask her to clarify, Rachel launched into a quick rundown of the attack on Marshall and her theory about Maggie. "But here's the thing that's going to nail the guy. He called me *Lieutenant*." If she hadn't been so focused on Marshall's pain, she'd have realized it earlier.

Thalia gasped, her mouth rounding into an O. She realized the truth, as well.

"It's someone in the company." Rich muttered something away from his phone's mic, then came back more clearly. "We can narrow the DNA search down to Slater's unit, and it might be enough for a judge to grant us emergency access, especially given the attack was on a federal agent. We can also cross-reference the current roster with whoever was deployed with Maggie Slater. If we get a hit, that's all we need, the ability to match one person's DNA to your evidence. Dana's calling Bradley now, and I'll forward the info you need to your team. Good catch, Blake."

Rachel almost sagged with relief, even though she knew there was a long night of digging through records ahead of her. "We could have this guy by tomorrow if we do this right."

Rich's voice cut through her thoughts. "Not so fast. You're assuming the guy hasn't gone AWOL. If his leave papers say he's one place and he's in the wind stalking Captain Slater, we won't have any idea where to look for him."

Rachel's momentary elation shattered on the floor like the cheap old-fashioned Christmas ball ornaments her grandmother had always hung on her tree. Their current line of thinking could only give them a name. Without a location, Marshall's stalker could still strike at any time, and Rachel couldn't risk her emotions getting in the way again. She was too close to the case now, emotionally involved, and protocol demanded she step away, whether she wanted to or not.

She dropped her head and closed her eyes. No matter how much she wanted to stay, she couldn't. "Thalia, head over to let Captain Slater know what we're working on." *And that I have no choice but to leave.*

When Thalia jogged out the door, Rachel closed it behind her. "Rich? There's one more thing we need to discuss."

THIRTEEN

Marshall shut the door behind Phillip and twisted the dead bolt. He checked it twice before he padded carefully to his recliner in his socks and dropped heavily into the comfort of his favorite chair. His legs didn't merely ache. They screamed with the kind of pain that said maybe Rachel was right and he should have them looked at. He didn't think anything was broken, but he had zero doubt that the pain would be more intense come morning.

Luckily for him, the army handed out ibuprofen like candy, so he had a decent supply in the medicine cabinet. He had a feeling he'd need it over the next few days.

The house was quiet. Wes was in the guest room, while Emma had conked out on the futon in the bonus room, excited by the prospect of "camping out" in her favorite space in the house. After all she'd been through, she deserved a "treat."

Marshall would bunk on the recliner or the couch if sleep ever came to him.

Except for the Christmas tree, the house was dark. Marshall stared at the red, white and green lights until they blurred in his tired eyes. Everything was off the rails. There was danger everywhere, from outside and inside.

It was clear that Emma was in love with the blue-eyed Captain Rachel. It was going to be hard on his daughter when she left.

Who was he kidding? It was going to be hard on him, but he refused to ruin her future by tying her to a man who would fail in the clinch, the same way he had tonight. Both of them could have been killed because he'd let an assailant sneak up and incapacitate him.

"You should get some sleep." The voice behind Marshall almost jerked him out of the chair. He'd have jumped up if his legs weren't already protesting.

Wes walked around between the fireplace and Marshall's chair, then settled onto the end of the sofa and propped his Christmas sock–covered feet up on the coffee table. Although Wes Brogden was knocking on the door of sixty, little gray tinseled his brown hair. Nearly thirty years in the military had left him fit and strong, and he'd maintained his strength even though retirement had come a decade earlier. His green eyes missed nothing, and they regarded Marshall as though Wes could read his mind.

Maggie and Emma both had his eyes. "Em looks so much like you, Wes."

"She's prettier than I'll ever be." Wes smiled and settled into the sofa as though he planned to stay awhile. "She's a great kid. I'm grateful you let me be a big part of her life."

"You're her grandfather." Marshall could feel his brow furrow. "Maggie's death didn't change that."

Wes nodded, the lights from the Christmas tree casting shadows on his face. They made him look as exhausted as Marshall felt. "You know my daughter's death wasn't your fault, right?"

Whoa. Okay. This was not the direction Marshall had expected the conversation to go. It echoed Rachel's words from the night before, the ones he'd battled ever since she'd spoken them. They went against everything he knew to be true. "She'd still be alive if I'd swallowed my pride that night. We all know that."

"Did you plan to handcuff Maggie to you? Keep her beside you twenty-four hours a day, seven days a week?" When Marshall sat forward to speak, Wes raised his hand to stop him. "The next morning, when you went to work, you wouldn't have been there. She'd have had opportunity then, too. And in that instance, my tiny little granddaughter would have been alone. I have never believed Maggie acted on impulse that night. What she did was not a spur-of-the-moment decision. You couldn't have stopped her, and you certainly didn't do anything to cause it."

Marshall dropped his head and propped his elbow on the arm of the recliner, burying his face in his hand. They'd never talked about the night Maggie had died. For four years, he'd assumed Wes blamed him as much as he blamed himself, but that he kept it inside so Marshall wouldn't stop him from seeing Emma.

Wes's words melded with Rachel's and went to war with everything he had believed for so long. His mind refused to surrender to another way of thinking. It was dangerous to believe this wasn't his fault, that he didn't need to be a better man, one more humble and less liable to put a woman like Rachel in danger if he dared to love her. "Don't talk like that." He kneaded his temple with his thumb, the words pounding against his skull.

"I was Maggie's husband. I was supposed to protect her. It was all on me, and I dropped the ball."

The silence stretched so long, Marshall lifted his head to see if Wes had somehow left the room without him noticing. But the man simply sat, staring at Marshall as though he'd suddenly started speaking Japanese.

Wes tilted his head to the side, started to speak, then stopped and continued to eye Marshall.

There was nothing more to say. Whatever false notions Wes had carried about Maggie and Marshall, they'd just been shattered. Marshall wouldn't blame the man if he walked out of this house forever. If he called the courts tomorrow and tried to wrest custody of his granddaughter away from the man who had failed to protect his daughter and, in recent days, had even failed to keep Emma safe.

The sofa squeaked, and the sound of Wes's breathing grew louder as he moved to the end of the couch closest to Marshall. There was a slight hesitation. Then he rested a heavy, warm hand on Marshall's shoulder. "Is that really what you believe? What you've been carrying all these years?"

"You mean, have I been carrying the truth

all these years?" Marshall dropped his hand from his face and pulled away from his father-in-law's grip. He'd get up and walk away if he thought his legs would hold him. "Yes." He spit the word out like a bullet. A bitter, angry bullet.

"Wow." Wes exhaled the word on a breath and sat back on the couch, crossing his arms. After a moment, he gripped his chin as though he was trying to make sure his words came out measured and right. "You deployed three times. Twice before you met Maggie and one shorter tour right after Emma was born."

That had nothing to do with anything, but Marshall nodded.

"Whose job was it to keep you safe when the bullets and the RPGs were flying?"

"Mine." It was a stupid question. Any soldier who'd been in combat knew that, and Wes had seen more action than Marshall had.

"Hmm." He stroked his chin. "And whose job was it to keep Maggie and Emma safe when you were gone those six months right after Em was born?"

Marshall moved to speak but stopped. From thousands of miles away on the far side of the world, there was nothing he could have done directly for them. There were times in those six months when the soldier had to take over the husband and father if he had any intention of getting home to them alive. At night, when he'd often fallen exhausted onto his cot, he'd sent up fervent prayers for his wife suffering from postpartum depression and PTSD and his new baby daughter. Back then, he'd trusted God with them and, truth be told, with himself, as well.

Everything had changed the morning he'd walked into the bedroom he shared with his wife and found her gone.

Wes slid to the edge of the couch and planted his elbows on his knees, leaning close to Marshall and keeping his voice low. "Marsh, you're not God. If you keep your fist closed around Emma, doing your human best to protect her from the world and every bad thing in it, trying to keep her from ever being sad or disappointed, you're going to crush her in the grip of your fear. Not only that, but you're going to leave her so sheltered that she can't function in the real world." Wes rose and laid a hand on Marshall's head, pausing for a long moment before he straightened. "You have a set of crutches in the garage, right? I thought I saw them when I was getting pizza out of the freezer."

"Yeah, from when I sprained my ankle on

a jump." His voice was low, his thoughts tied up in everything Wes had said and everything Rachel had tried to tell him the night before.

"I'm going to get them. Might help you get around a little bit easier." His father-in-law walked toward the kitchen but stopped in the doorway. "I know we're two days from Christmas Eve. I know you want to stay home and not upend Emma's world, and I'm not trying to overstep my grandfatherly bounds by telling you what to do. But I will say that I'd sleep a lot easier if the two of you were safe somewhere other than here until Captain Blake and her people can find whoever did this to you." He disappeared into the kitchen, and the door to the garage closed softly behind him a moment later.

Marshall sat back in the chair and stared at the ceiling. He'd done his fair share of praying over the years. Believed he trusted God. But everything Wes had said banged against his skull with a physical throb that timed with his heartbeat.

There had been a time in his life when he'd laid everything at God's feet and trusted Him to take care of it. Marshall had done his part. Had been responsible and handled the things he had to, but he hadn't tried to shoulder the burden of everyone else's choices and of everyone else's happiness.

Until Maggie had died.

After that, he'd tried to control everything and everyone in his world.

Something snapped in his chest, the weight of years of grief and blame falling away. His father-in-law was right. With Maggie's death, he'd not only taken on a responsibility and a guilt that had never been his to bear, he'd also walled up his life and Emma's in a prison of fear. Fear that he'd fail her. Fear that he'd cause her harm. Fear that, if he blinked even for a second, his daughter would vanish. And while, at this moment, that was a real possibility, God still had his little girl in His hand.

Doing the right thing for her meant laying his fear down and letting her feel the disappointment of another journey to North Carolina. Letting her grow into a healthy individual who understood that life wasn't always happy, but it would always have joy if God was in the picture.

It meant forgiving himself for his mistakes and freeing his heart to love someone else.

Someone like Rachel.

He dropped the foot of the recliner and sat forward in the seat. Where was his father-in-law with those crutches? He needed to talk to

Rachel, not only to coordinate a run for the safe house, but also to tell her he was letting go of the past and looking to a new future... maybe with her.

A rustle in the kitchen almost brought him to his feet, but it was Thalia who walked into the living room, not Wes.

She looked straight at him with a look that chilled something in his newly warmed heart. Pulling in a deep breath, she finally spoke. "Marshall? Rachel's gone."

Rachel dropped her duffel bag by the apartment door and headed for the bedroom to grab her suitcase, glancing around as she went. The corporate apartment she'd lived in for the past few months had come furnished, so all she'd brought along were clothes and a few personal items. Everything fit into a duffel, a large suitcase and a backpack. She'd traveled light, never expecting to stay so long.

Certainly never expecting to leave part of her heart behind with the company commander who'd initially been her prime suspect.

Everything was moving too quickly. When she'd confessed her feelings for Marshall to Rich, he'd pulled her off the investigation. She wasn't even allowed to dig into records.

He'd ordered her back to Camp McGee immediately.

Marshall would be hurt when he figured out she'd left town without saying goodbye. And Emma? Rachel stopped at the bedroom door and rested her hand on the wooden frame. She hoped the excitement of Christmas would stem some of Emma's disappointment over the fact that Captain Rachel had left.

It was easier this way, at least in the long run. She'd left a note and her present for the little girl behind, a stuffed army bear she'd picked up at the P/X. As much as she'd wanted to slip into the house and tell Em goodbye, the little girl was already asleep. Waking her would have made everything harder on them both.

As for Marshall, he had his own issues to work through, issues that could keep him from ever falling in love again, or at least admitting to himself that he had. If this were truly about Maggie and Emma, a lot of old wounds could get ripped open that would set him back for years. And her job was based at a training post in North Carolina where an active, adventurous infantryman like himself would have no job to do. One of them would have to sacrifice their calling if they were going to be together. She wouldn't ask that of him, and she knew him well enough to know he'd never ask that of her, either.

Grabbing her pillow from the bed, she flipped off the light and headed up the short hallway to throw her things into her rental car. It was late and she was tired, but she'd drive as far as she could go tonight. All she knew was that she had to get out of the area before she defied a direct order, pointed her car in the direction of Marshall's house and gave herself over to the lie that they could make this work. That her future could embrace him and Emma.

She flipped off the light in the spare bedroom, where Thalia had dropped her things. Thalia and Phillip would take turns staying here until the new team arrived to take over.

At Camp McGee, Rachel would head up what needed to be finalized to wrap up the indictment against Plyler. That had been her job from the beginning. It was the one she'd finish now. Marshall and Emma would fall under someone else's care until Overwatch could prove they were safe.

A soft sound from the entry stilled her steps. Sounded like a key in the lock. Thalia and Phillip had spare keys to the apartment since they were all bunking here, but they ought to be at Marshall's house, keeping an eye on the family.

Dropping her pillow, Rachel rested her palm on the grip of her pistol at her hip and prepared to take a stand as the door swung open.

Marshall hobbled in, resting heavily on a pair of crutches.

Her heart thunked heavily in her chest, a jolt of electricity at the sight of him. He was decked out in gray plaid flannel pants and a green long-sleeved Henley, likely what he'd planned to sleep in tonight.

It was too much. Reason threatened to flee at the sight of him. "What are you doing here?" But she knew. Thalia had ratted out Rachel, then handed over her key. There was no other explanation. Despite her earlier assertions and her natural bent toward cynicism, the younger soldier was a romantic at heart.

But she had no idea what she was meddling in.

Glancing from her bags, then up to her, Marshall shoved the door shut with one of his crutches and stood in the small hardwood entryway, eyeing her across the space of the open living room. "I could ask the same thing." He sounded tired and maybe angry.

Or hurt.

As his gaze held hers, Rachel had no doubt. It was hurt, and she'd caused it. All the more reason for her to leave as soon as possible.

"I have to go back to Camp McGee. I talked to my chain of command earlier. I've been pulled off the investigation due to my... emotional involvement. Phillip and Thalia will watch over you and Emma, and another team will be sent as soon as possible." *Wait.* She narrowed her eyes. "Did you come over here by yourself?"

"Thalia gave me your key. She followed me here, but I sent her back to my house to help Phillip keep an eye on Emma. I told her I was safe with you."

He was safe with her? Well, that just proved he wasn't thinking straight. Neither one of them was safe with each other. Her willingness to ignore the danger and take that little jaunt to the river walk tonight had proved it. Snatching her pillow from the floor, she steeled herself against him and stalked toward the door, which he blocked. "I have to go. I have a job to do back at McGee. You have an entirely different assignment, and you have to think about Emma. She needs to be your primary concern." He had no idea how much he needed to be concerned about his child, and she couldn't tell him yet, not until they had solid proof. "You need to take up the team on the offer of going to the safe house. Now." It was the best she could give him.

"You may be right about all that, but she's not my only concern." With one crutch, he shoved her duffel bag to the side and stepped around it. His eyes caught hers and held. He came toward her with the kind of determination she'd grown used to seeing when he dealt with his soldiers.

But never with her. There was something different about him. Something that said he wasn't backing down the way he had the night before. While something had smoothed the worried furrows around his eyes, his stance spoke of a man who would not back away again.

He stopped a mere two feet away from her, and, just like she'd feared, she couldn't back away, either. "Why did you come here?" Her words lost every inch of the power she'd been determined to put behind them. "This would have been so much easier if you hadn't."

"If I hadn't, you'd have left without giving me the chance to tell you some things." His voice was as low as hers, but it held a strength hers didn't. "Important things."

She could see it in his expression even before he said it. He was about to say everything her heart wanted to hear and wanted to say in return. Things she'd dream of long after she'd left this place—and him—behind.

He'd be her biggest regret, but there was nothing else he could be.

Pulling in a deep breath, Rachel stepped back, drawing on reserves she didn't even know she had. *Lord, help me to leave. Give me strength. This can't end well for either of us.*

"I have to go." She stepped around him and walked to the door, shouldering her backpack. "I'll call Thalia and wait in the parking lot for her to come back and get you."

"You're leaving because you're scared."

His voice held a certainty that grated against her raw nerves. "I'm leaving because I was ordered to." Her voice held authority, but she stopped with her hand wrapped around the handle of her suitcase, staring at the back of the door. Scared? Of what? Of hurting him? Yes. Of one of them eventually resenting the other because they gave up their career? Yes.

She straightened her shoulders and reached for the doorknob again.

But Marshall wasn't finished. "Your first

marriage was a wreck. I get that. You loved him, and he threw your love back at you."

Rachel dug her teeth into her lower lip. He wasn't playing fair. This had nothing to do with her past.

"You can package up your fears any way you want to, Rachel, but they will never be the truth." There was a thunk and a shuffle as he eased his way closer. When he spoke again, his voice was right behind her, and she could almost feel the warmth of his chest against her back. "You can say you don't want us to resent each other or that we have different careers. You can even say that I have too much baggage, which I probably do. But so do you. When you look at me, you see him. You see that I used to drink too much, and you see him. You're scared I'll fall back into that. Scared I'll walk away from you for someone else. Scared I won't protect you because your first husband didn't protect you."

His words cut through the layers she'd built around her heart, slicing to her core. Was he right? Was she making excuses? Terrified of being less than enough? "You're the one who's scared you'll fail to protect." She winced at the bite in her words.

"Not anymore." There was no hesitation in his declaration. He stood so close to her that the words blew warm against the back of her neck. "I'll mess up because I'm human. There's no way around it. But I will always do my best to protect you. You're worth all that and more."

His truth washed across iced-over places in her heart, warming them for the first time since she'd learned about Robert's infidelity. If she wanted, she could lean back against Marshall and pretend that there was no danger outside the door. That they could make this all work.

She shook her head as though she could shake the thought. Just because he'd shown up on her doorstep with a plan to win her over didn't mean he was right.

It didn't mean any of this was right.

Without turning to look at him, she pulled her phone from her pocket and dialed. When Thalia answered, she swallowed the pain that threatened to choke her into silence. "It's Rachel. I need you to turn around right now and come get Marshall."

"I... Okay." Thalia sounded as though it was the last thing she wanted to do, but they could discuss how personal lives should never interfere with protocol later. "I can be there in five. I'm not that far away."

Rachel killed the call and shoved the phone

into her hip pocket. Without daring to look at Marshall, she tightened her grip on her suitcase, then hefted her backpack higher on her shoulder and picked up her duffel bag.

She pulled the door open. "I have to go. Lock the dead bolt behind me. I'll wait in the parking lot until Thalia gets here to make sure you're safe."

"Rachel, don't do this."

Ignoring him, she stepped out the door and shut it firmly behind her, then headed for the outside stairs as fast as a soldier loaded down with her gear could go.

Her suitcase bumped down the cement-and-metal stairs behind her. *Lord, let him see reason. He's wrong about me. About us. Don't let him follow me. We can't do this. He can't resent me. I can't resent him. We can't.*

Clicking the button to pop the trunk, Rachel swiped at warm tears that ran down her cheeks. She hadn't even realized she was crying. Rounding the car, she dropped her duffel and her backpack inside, then bent to hoist her suitcase as her phone buzzed in her pocket. *What now?*

Running footsteps from the left caused her to straighten and turn, but the figure coming at her caught her off balance. He shoved her in the stomach and knocked her against the trunk.

Rachel struggled and tried to cry out, but her awkward position and the man's weight over her kept her pinned into a painful side bend. He pressed one hand tight over her mouth and jerked her head to the side, exposing her neck.

There was a jab and a pinch at the side of her neck. She tried to wriggle free, but her limbs grew too heavy. The world swam in murk. Like swimming underwater.

Then darkness.

FOURTEEN

Marshall leaned heavily on his crutches and stared at the door. She'd actually walked out on him. Walked out and closed the door on everything they could have together.

Because she was scared. It had come to him in a blinding flash while she was talking. This had nothing to do with their careers. Nothing to do with his past and his failings. The root of her argument was her fear of their relationship ending with her in pain.

And the root of that fear was her ex-husband's cruel betrayal. It was possible she saw a glimpse of him in Marshall's former drinking habit, so she was running.

Marshall braced himself and stood taller. Well, she didn't get to unilaterally wipe out their future. He was going to do the one thing her former husband never did.

He was going to fight for her.

Jerking the door open, he hopped his

crutches onto the landing and headed for the stairs, dreading the slow creep to the bottom. It would be faster to sit and scoot his way down the steps than it would be to walk it, but his dignity wouldn't allow it.

Gripping the handrail and grimacing against the pain, he took one step and was about to take another when a car door slammed and tires squealed in the parking lot. He looked up just in time to see the blue sedan Rachel had been driving careen around the corner of the next building at a speed he'd never thought her capable of outside of a high-speed chase.

He sank to the top step and propped his crutches beside him. Even if he could get down the steps at normal speed and without pain, he'd never be able to catch her without endangering his own life. The one thing he could never forget, no matter how he felt about Rachel, was that he was Emma's only living parent.

He should do what she'd said and get back into the apartment behind a locked door until Thalia arrived, but the pain of overexertion and overworked ibuprofen staged a revolt that shot from his shins all the way through his body. He might not even be able to stand again without help.

Marshall pounded his fist against the concrete step, the blow making a hollow sound in the metal frame of the staircase and sending a ragged pain up his arm. He couldn't even chase down the woman he loved. Maybe he was wrong before. Maybe Wes was wrong. Maybe he really wasn't capable of doing this the right way.

Except he knew he was. He'd prayed the whole way here. He'd felt the unaccustomed quiet in the deepest part of him. This wasn't his fault. He wasn't unworthy of a woman like Rachel or a daughter like Emma.

God said so.

Leaning to the side, Marshall pulled his phone from his hip pocket and dialed Rachel's number. She might have a wildly fast head start on him, but he had her number. He could blow up her phone all night until she answered.

Straight to voice mail.

He was dialing again when headlights cruised into the lot in front of the building and Thalia's rental car slid into a space beside his SUV, under a streetlight. After a quick glance, Marshall dialed again.

Voice mail.

Thalia took the stairs two at a time, phone in hand. "Where's Rachel?"

"She left." He didn't look up. Didn't want

to see the pity on her face. Instead, like the desperate, lovesick fool Rachel had turned him into, he redialed. One ring. Two—

Thalia snatched the phone from his hand and killed the call. "Captain Slater." Her voice was so sharp it snatched his gaze up to hers. "Where. Is. Rachel?"

"I told you. She left." Wait. Thalia looked pale. Her eyebrows were drawn together. She was definitely not her typical put-together self. "What's going on?"

"I don't know. But she's not answering her phone."

"I realize that. I was trying to call her." He snatched his phone out of her grasp. "She left in a hurry."

"She left you alone?" Thalia shook her head, her forehead creasing into deep furrows.

"I guess so. She said she was going to wait for you to get here before she headed out, but she took off out of here so quickly that she left rubber on the asphalt at the corner." Which was not like her at all. Suddenly, Marshall felt the weight of Thalia's concern. While Rachel was upset and on the run from her feelings for him, she'd never leave him alone and vulnerable. "Something's not right."

"You think?" Thalia flipped over her phone

and pressed the screen. "I tried to call her less than two minutes after she called me. No answer. She never doesn't answer, not when there's a case on the line and we're waiting on intel." She glanced at Marshall and looked back at the screen.

"You know who's after me." Marshall shoved up to stand. "You know who the DNA belonged to." Marshall's heart beat faster. He was about to find out who was after him, who had tried to terrorize his daughter.

"Sergeant Wylie Joseph."

"Joseph?" Marshall grabbed his chin and dragged his hand down his neck, trying to hold on to the idea that the new team leader in his company had not only attacked Rachel in his backyard but had also likely been the man to threaten and attack him. To try to steal his daughter. "Why?"

Thalia gripped her phone tighter, but she lifted her chin and pegged his gaze. She eyed him for a long moment as though she was weighing the words before she spoke them.

"Just tell me. This involves me and my daughter. Talk."

"We only have speculation, but..." Thalia softened slightly. "Seven years ago, Wylie Joseph was stationed at the same FOB in Afghanistan as Maggie."

What did that have to do with…? *No.* A wave of nausea broke over Marshall with a crash that nearly doubled him over at the waist. She couldn't be saying that.

"Captain Slater, I spoke to Joseph's former commanding officer. He said a female in the unit asked to speak to him about Joseph, but shortly after that she had a breakdown of some sort and had to be sent back to the United States. Whatever she wanted to say was never pursued."

"Maggie." Marshall couldn't get enough air. There wasn't enough in the small space between him and Thalia. With the last of his reserves, he shoved past her and inched his way down the stairs, desperate for space and for freedom. Desperate to outrun the thoughts that pounded his brain. Maggie raped. Joseph responsible. One of his own trusted soldiers responsible.

Captain, you stole my life… I'll have it back.

At the bottom of the stairs, Marshall gulped air, spent from exertion and emotion. This could not be real. A man he'd worked beside, had greeted every day as a soldier in his chain of command, had invited into his home… That man had raped the woman who would become his wife.

That man was the biological father of his child.

Leaning heavily against the truck, he bent forward on the crutches, trying to grasp a truth that refused to be grasped. He'd thought he knew pain, but this was a ripping tear that was so much worse. So much more—

Something glinted in the parking space where Rachel's car had been, dragging his attention off himself. He leaned forward, battling nausea and fear and anger.

An empty syringe gleamed in the streetlight. Behind it, her backpack lay tumbled on the ground.

"Phillip tracked her phone and found it on the side of Wilma Rudolph Boulevard, not far from the apartment. The police are on scene at the apartment. Captain Slater and I are back at his house." From the den, Thalia's voice drifted into the kitchen. She was speaking quietly into her phone, but there was no way Marshall could avoid hearing her in the silent house.

He braced his elbows on the kitchen table and buried his head in his hands, digging his fingers into the side of his head.

The wood pattern on the tabletop jumped with every beat of his heart. He closed his eyes, but even the darkness pulsed with the rhythm. The beat featured two syllables. *Failure*. Over and over again, the word pounded against his skull.

"We're going to need a rush on that second team." Thalia was still talking, but her voice grew closer. When Marshall lifted his head, she was standing in the kitchen entry, watching him. She spoke into the phone, but the words were aimed at him. "When that team gets here, Phillip and I will escort the *entire* Slater family to the safe house."

No arguments. No discussion. She'd forcibly wrest him out of his house if need be to keep Marshall, Emma and Wes safe.

His family had to come first. *Emma* had to come first. But the thought of leaving Clarksville while Rachel was in the custody of a man who was clearly out to cause Marshall pain... A man who had not hesitated to hurt Maggie in the past...

The thought shuddered through him, a nightmare from which he couldn't wake up.

He turned and stared at the closed blinds, then shoved his chair away from the table, grabbed his crutches and crept his way past Thalia. If he sat still any longer, he'd blow into tiny pieces. He had to get moving, to stop the past atrocities and the present what-ifs from cycling through his mind.

There must be something he could do. Rachel had been missing for two hours. Sitting still in a kitchen chair was ripping his heart out.

How the rest of the house slept through their ins and outs and his pacing was beyond him. He'd considered waking Wes, but then they'd all be tripping over each other. Wes would try to be helpful in a situation where there was no help.

Except prayer. His dialogue with God hadn't stopped since the horrible truth of Rachel's disappearance had become evident. The words weren't necessarily intelligible, but his soul screamed pleas to his creator, the cries of an aching heart.

A heart that ached as badly as his legs did. From the foot of the stairs he stared at the top, desperate to see his daughter. He might not know what was happening to Rachel, but there might be peace in seeing that Emma was safely tucked beneath the blankets on the futon. He needed that peace desperately.

Abandoning one crutch against the wall, he made his way slowly up the stairs, gripping the second crutch and the hand railing for all he was worth. This night involved way too much climbing and not enough energy.

At the top, he paused to catch his breath and let his legs rest. Then he made his way up the hallway to the bonus room and eased the door open.

The dim glow of a princess night-light cast warm shadows into the room. On the unfolded futon, Emma slept flat on her back in a tangle of blankets and stuffed animals, both arms flung over her head.

Someone had told him once that a kid who slept sprawled out like that felt safe. If that was the case, after all Emma had been through as a toddler, then he must have done his job as a father. His little girl clearly trusted that her daddy would protect her.

Emma's sprawl was a far cry from how Maggie had typically slept, curled into a ball, her face always turned toward the door, presumably so that no one could sneak up on her in the night.

Marshall eased into the rocking chair closest to the futon and watched his daughter sleep. What had Maggie suffered through that he hadn't been able to see from the outside? For the first time, he understood how she could feel so helpless against forces she couldn't see to fight. He wanted to run into the darkness and disappear, to bury himself under blankets and never crawl out of bed again. Something deep inside said that was exactly how Maggie had felt, only there was nowhere for her to hide from the enemy inside her own mind.

Her death wasn't his fault, but he could have been more understanding when she was struggling. It might not have saved her life, but his patience could have made her too-short life more peaceful.

He'd definitely be more sympathetic with his daughter. Tougher than he had been in the past, enforcing more boundaries, but more sympathetic.

He spent a few minutes in the quiet with only the sound of Emma's breathing. He prayed for his daughter, for what to do with the knowledge of who her biological father was, for Rachel's safety…

He couldn't sit here idle while she was in danger. If her team was working and the police were working, he should be, too. Maybe if he drove around town he'd see something they didn't. He'd already given them everything he had on Joseph on his work laptop. They'd dispatched MPs to his quarters on post. Phillip was there with them looking for clues, but there was no sign of Rachel or of Sergeant Joseph.

With a last long look at his daughter, Marshall eased up and left the room, closing the door quietly behind him. She needed her sleep tonight if they were going to cram her back into a car tomorrow for another wild run to North Carolina.

He was halfway to the stairs when his phone vibrated in his pocket. Leaning on his one crutch, he thumbed the screen to open an incoming text, heart picking up a beat. It had better be news about Rachel. *Let them have found her safely, Lord.* This prayer, finally, had words instead of simply emotions.

The number wasn't one he recognized. I have your girlfriend. Will trade her for you. I don't plan to hurt Emma, but I will if cops show. Leave your cell phone. You won't need it. There's a rental parked at the end of your street. Keys in glove box. GPS programmed.

The phone buzzed again, and this time a photo appeared. It was grainy, as though it had been taken with a low-end phone camera, likely a burner. The flash was too bright, the surroundings too dark. But Rachel slumped forward in a foldable canvas camping chair, her feet bound to the legs, her hands tied behind her.

Marshall closed his eyes and drew a deep breath slowly as his heart pounded and his vision swam. His fingers tightened on the phone. He closed the screen again. The sight of it was more than he could bear.

Pivoting, he looked at the door to the bonus room, then to the stairs. If he went on this fool's errand, Sergeant Wylie Joseph would almost certainly kill him, leaving Emma fatherless and vulnerable. If he didn't go, there was no doubt Rachel would die in his place. If he notified Thalia, then Joseph would kill Rachel and come after Emma.

Laying his phone on the overhang railing, Marshall limped painfully toward the stairs. The only way to end this was to sacrifice himself.

FIFTEEN

A dull throbbing at the base of Rachel's skull thrummed a beat against the blackness. She was bent forward, her body weight pulling painfully at her shoulders. Her neck pinched and stung.

Her eyes refused to open at first, but when they did, the world blurred between dim light and dark shadow. Nothing seemed to form into a clear object.

It was cold. The chill pressed against her skin until it seemed to ice her bones. Her head pounded with the rhythm of her heart.

So much cold.

So much pain.

Rachel tried to lift her head and press a hand to her temple, but her arms were stuck behind her. Panic quickened her heartbeat and the pounding against her skull. She lurched, but something at her wrists cut and burned, then slicked. Blood. She was bleeding.

"Good to see you're awake, *Lieutenant*." The male voice from her left barely penetrated the pain. It brought back a rush of memory. Her suitcase in the trunk. The weight of someone holding her down. The stinging pain in her neck.

She sucked in a deep breath of damp, cold air and jerked her head up, her vision darkening from the pain and the sudden movement. The room spun but then, like a top, seemed to settle into a watery view.

A man stepped closer and knelt in front of her, resting his hands on her knees.

She wanted to recoil, but her legs were bound to the chair as tightly as her wrists.

He leaned forward so that his face came into view.

Her sharp inhalation knifed through her lungs. "Joseph." For a quick instant, rescue fluttered through her mind. He was one of her soldiers. How had he found her?

But then his hands tightened on her knees, and he sneered with a look that dismissed her pain. "Actually, I've been calling you the wrong rank for too long, right, *Captain*?"

He knew. How did he know? Her eyes skittered from his face to her hip. Her holster was empty. Her jacket was missing. Her jacket, where her badge and ID rested in the interior pocket.

Joseph leaned to one side, still way too close to her personal space, and pulled something from his hip pocket, keeping that one hand on her knee. He held up the case that contained her identification and flipped it open inches from her face. "Captain Rachel Blake. Military intelligence." He flipped the case closed and shoved it back into his pocket. "Were you assigned to protect Slater?"

It was tough to follow his train of thought. Whatever he'd injected her with must have done a number on her. It was like thinking through thick fog. "From you? You think pretty highly of yourself."

"So it's purely coincidence that you were around? That you were one of the team of agents keeping Slater safe?" He stroked a thumb along her cheek.

The urge to flinch away from him was strong, but she wouldn't give him the satisfaction of having the upper hand. "Why would military intelligence be looking for you?" Her tongue was thick and her mouth dry. The words tripped on their way out.

Hard brown eyes searched hers for a long moment, as if he were trying to read what she was thinking.

She refused to look away and she also refused to vomit, which was exactly what the combination of drugs and his touch were about to bring to pass. If she projected strength and kept him on his toes, he might start talking just to keep his own macho bravado in place.

Laughing, he tapped his index finger on the end of her nose like she was a child and stood, walking a few feet away.

Finally, she could breathe without the woodsy smell of high-end cologne wafting past her nose. She might never want to breathe in that scent again after this was all over.

With that space, Rachel was able to take in her surroundings. A lantern flashlight sat on a foldable plastic camping table about ten feet away, casting heavy shadows against stone walls. They must be in one of the small caves that dotted the landscape around Clarksville. That explained the chill. "Sergeant, where's my jacket?"

Joseph didn't answer. He glanced at his watch, walked to the edge of the light and stared toward what must be the mouth of the cave. The light was bluer there, as though starlight or moonlight tried to encroach on their hideout. The cave wasn't deep.

Still, screaming probably wouldn't help. It was doubtful anyone lived nearby, and the sound would only echo off the walls and make Joseph angry. Right now he was calm—likely because he had a plan in the works, one she needed to figure out if she were going to get out of here and save Marshall.

One thing at a time. She had to get her mind out of this fog and off her emotions. Spiraling into panic wouldn't dig her out of this mess. It would only give Sergeant Joseph all the power. She had to focus, to ground herself in her surroundings before she could even consider finding a way out.

She scanned the space again, working her arms against what felt like the jagged edges of zip ties. All she got for her trouble was a deeper pain and the slick of her own blood against her skin. On the table, her sidearm lay next to the lantern, tantalizingly close but entirely too far away.

With another glance at his watch, Joseph came back and stood in front of her.

Rachel held his gaze. She would show no fear. "You didn't answer my question." What she wouldn't give for some water right now to rinse the cotton from her mouth and to slake the raw scratch in her throat.

"Intelligence has no reason to investigate me. I haven't done anything wrong." Something slid across his expression that dulled the arrogance he'd walked with since she'd first realized who he was. Something that looked like pain. "If you're looking for villains, you need to look at your boyfriend."

"I think you're mistaking my professional relationship with Captain Slater for something else." This man could never know what had happened between her and Marshall. He could never know that Marshall Slater had found his way into her heart. In Joseph's hands, that knowledge could lead to disaster.

Kneeling in front of her, Joseph tilted his head to one side and regarded her. "You're lying." He stood and walked toward the entrance, once again checking his watch. "At first, I was confused, because he's too buttoned-up to fraternize with a subordinate in his own company. But with you both being the same rank, it makes sense. I've seen the way he looks at you and you look at him. Maggie and I had that once." Sniffing, Joseph turned his head toward the ceiling, the lantern's shadows deepening the planes of his face. With a sudden turn, he stalked back and glared down at her. "Slater killed her. You know that, right?"

This time, Rachel couldn't bury her emotions. Her suspicions had been correct. Horribly correct. The shock and revulsion had to be all over her face. Sergeant Wylie Joseph was the faceless soldier who'd raped Maggie overseas. He was Emma's blood father.

"I'm going to raise the daughter I didn't even know I had until I saw the photo of the three of them on Slater's desk. That picture… Maggie with him. And with my daughter between them. He had my family."

He dared to call his violence toward Maggie *love*. To think he could parent a precious child like Emma. "No." Rachel spit the word out with all the bitterness it deserved. If it had physical power, it would have burned his skin raw.

The rage that reddened Joseph's face revealed the murderous depths of his delusions. He drew his fist back, ready to strike.

"Don't." The command was harsh and authoritative, echoing off the walls of the small cave.

Marshall. He stood at the mouth of the cave, leaning heavily on his crutches. His expression burned with anger and pain.

No.

He couldn't be here. Joseph would kill both of them.

Smirking, Joseph lowered his hand and walked around to stand behind Rachel. "I really didn't expect you to show."

"I'm here, Sergeant. You can let her go." Marshall sounded weary beneath the force in his voice. It was doubtful that Joseph would notice, but it was evident in his tone and in his stance. "This is between me and you."

"And she means a lot to you." Joseph shifted, and something dug into the base of Rachel's skull.

The unmistakable chill of the barrel of a pistol.

There was nothing Marshall could do. He was helpless. Even on his best days in top physical shape, he couldn't close the fifteen-foot gap between Rachel and himself faster than Joseph could pull the trigger and destroy their future.

All he had was his mind. It had better work faster if this was going to end with them alive at the end of this.

There had to be an end to this. Tonight.

He gripped the crutches tighter and tried not to lean on them as much as his shaking legs wanted to. The rocky walk from the road to the small cave had sapped what was left of his strength, but he could never let

Joseph know that. He forced what little reserve he had left into his voice. "I know why you're doing this." His voice rang back to him against the damp rock walls.

"Because you killed Maggie." The sheer hatred in Joseph's gaze was unlike anything Marshall had ever faced. It nearly buried him on the spot.

Easing a step deeper into the cave, trying to formulate a plan, Marshall kept his gaze locked on Joseph's. "Up until yesterday, I'd have agreed with you about that."

Joseph's cheek muscle flinched. The words had hit home. Marshall had to keep him talking, had to keep Joseph focused on him so that he didn't turn his attention to Rachel and the pistol's trigger.

Please, Lord... Marshall pleaded another desperate, wordless prayer. He couldn't do this alone. For too long he'd tried to control everything. And now? Now he had to release it and loft it higher than himself.

He hobbled another cautious step, fighting to keep his eyes off Rachel. For one thing, it would never escape Joseph's notice.

For the other, Marshall had to maintain his own sanity. If he allowed himself to take in the full extent of the gravity and danger in the situation, he'd never be able to keep up the bravado. Joseph was a loose cannon and there was no telling when he'd fire. "What exactly do you want from me, Sergeant? My life? My daughter?"

"She's my daughter!" Joseph's roar bounced around the cave, pounding Marshall's ears with the multiple echoes of his rage. He jerked the gun up toward Marshall, knocking Rachel forward as the barrel raked the back of her head.

She grunted with the pain and kept her head low, bent forward as far as her bound hands would let her.

Marshall could see straight down the barrel of the pistol. Not a place he ever wanted to be.

But this was infinitely better than having death pressed point-blank against Rachel's skull.

He tore his gaze from the weapon. Too many people focused on the weapon and not on the way out. He had to find the way out.

He met Rachel's gaze. Far from revealing the pain he'd expected, she looked determined.

Her eyes shifted from his to the side, slowly, deliberately, then came back to his. She drew her mouth tight.

"She's not your daughter. She's mine. Mine

and Maggie's. Do you know how it felt to see your happy family in that photo on your desk? How it felt to have wondered where Maggie was for all these years, only to find out she'd been with you? Living with a child that she never told me we had?" Joseph's voice broke the flow of the silent conversation, calling Marshall's attention back to the gun that wavered between them. "You do not get to raise my child. You do not get to have my life."

"Your life?" This guy was off the chain. Marshall had to stop this. Soon. He let his gaze wander the cave, sliding past where Rachel's had drifted.

His heart nearly stopped. Not six feet away, on a small portable camping table next to the lantern that provided the only light, rested her sidearm.

He let his eyes keep moving, not letting Joseph know what he'd seen, and kept himself from giving any meaningful look to Rachel. If he could just get there... Did he dare make Joseph angrier? The man would either scream out his story or pull the trigger.

What choice did he have? "This isn't some love story, Sergeant. You raped her."

"No." The gun wavered. "We were supposed to be together. She needed to understand she was mine."

Marshall wanted to rush the guy and beat him senseless. This was sick. So sick. "You stalked her and harassed her until she complained to your chain of command. You hurt her." He eased another step closer and fought to keep the tremor of his emotions out of his voice. "She suffered because of what you did to her."

"That's a lie!" Joseph's ragged scream pounded through the cave as he shouted at the ceiling.

Marshall leveraged off his crutch and dived for the table.

Rachel threw herself backward, driving herself and the chair into Joseph as the pistol fired wildly.

The table fell, the flashlight bulb shattered and Rachel's gun clattered across the floor as the cave plunged into darkness.

Marshall scrambled for the pistol on the rocky floor as Joseph shouted nearly unintelligible curses into the darkness. There was another wild pistol shot.

A grunt came from the entrance to the cave, and then a light illuminated the area. A female voice rang out. "Military intelligence. Drop the weapon. Now!"

Thalia. Somehow, Thalia had found them. Which meant Phillip was nearby, as well.

In the beam of her flashlight, Joseph squinted, then raised his weapon directly at her position.

Another shot.

Joseph fell into the darkness.

Marshall slumped, caught his breath, then pushed himself onto his side. Rachel. Why hadn't she said anything? "Thalia. I need light."

Keeping his eyes away from where Joseph lay, he found the wall and pulled himself up, then limped painfully to where Rachel lay on her side in the chair, her eyes closed. He dropped to his backside beside her. "Rach?"

"It's over?" Her eyes opened and met his, clear and uninjured.

Marshall exhaled the breath he'd been holding for days and pushed the hair out of her eyes. "I think so."

"Thalia should have a knife." Her voice was hoarse and dry, but he got the meaning. Cut her loose. Get her out of here. Now.

Phillip dropped to his knees beside them, wielding a flashlight and pulling a knife from his belt. "Let's get you out of here. Local law enforcement is on the way. So are the EMTs." He stopped with the knife poised to cut Rachel free. "I'm only cutting you loose if you agree to let them take a look at you."

The look she lasered on Phillip should have melted him on the spot. While the young sergeant didn't collapse into a puddle, he did get moving and free his team leader from the bonds that held her. Phillip helped her to her feet as Marshall leveraged his crutches to rise and limp out beside her. "How did you find us?"

"Smart move unlocking your phone and leaving it out in the open. Thalia found it and traced the number on the texts from Joseph."

Just like he'd hoped she would.

"You just better say a whole lot of prayers of thanks she found it as quickly as she did."

"I have no idea what you're talking about. Both of you have a story to tell me." Rachel stumbled and Phillip caught her, supporting her with an arm around her back.

They were a pair, her leaning heavily on Phillip as though she couldn't quite maintain her balance and Marshall hobbling along on crutches beside her.

But at least they were alive.

SIXTEEN

As Phillip helped Rachel settle on a large rock at the head of the short trail that led down from the road, she turned toward the mouth of the cave. "Where's Thalia?" Normally she'd be the first one to Rachel's side, having been on the team longer than Phillip. Those wild gunshots and Thalia's absence grated against her already-frayed nerves.

"She's fine. She's dealing with Sergeant Joseph." He stepped away from them as Marshall settled next to Rachel. "If you're fine to wait here for the local folks, I'll go back and help her."

"She wasn't hit?"

Phillip shook his head, backing toward the mouth of the cave.

Maybe he was telling the truth and maybe he wasn't, but there was no way to know unless she trusted him. Rachel nodded her assent. The motion set the world into a wavy spin, and she wobbled slightly as Phillip turned and jogged away. She leaned heavily against Marshall's shoulder. How was he here beside her?

He slipped an arm around her, seeming to need her support as much as she needed his. "You okay?"

"I will be." She nestled against him, trying to grasp that, although they sat in the darkness waiting for local law enforcement to blaze up, they were safe. It was actually over. "Whatever he shot me up with is taking its time to wear off."

"He drugged you?" Marshall's arm tightened around her, and even the air around him seemed to charge with anger and concern.

"I'll be fine. Whatever it was, it obviously didn't kill me."

It was several deep breaths later before he relaxed slightly, but his hold on her didn't ease. "You know he would have killed you eventually."

"I'd have managed to find a way out of it." She'd never been in a situation that she hadn't been able to escape before. Always, she'd managed to survive, and she'd have found a way this time. At the moment, her muddled mind and exhausted body just weren't sure how. It wasn't a reality she wanted to dwell on, but she knew from past experience that she wouldn't rest until she'd puzzled out the plan that would have led to her survival without Marshall endangering his life for her.

"His plan was to kill both of us, and you played right into it." She sat up and pulled away from him, clasping her hands in her lap. "You shouldn't have come. I had it under control."

"You were tied to a chair. Unarmed. Drugged."

"Stop." The harsh word chilled the already-cold night air, born of a rush of fear. His words threw her back into the cave, back into helplessness with a man who had raped Marshall's wife and had proved himself capable of murder.

She didn't need him reminding her of how close she'd come to losing her life at Joseph's hand. Three times. If she had the balance, she'd walk away.

Except she really didn't want to.

As if he knew what she was thinking, Marshall slipped his other arm around her and pulled her closer, cradling her. Her head rested against his chest, where the thump of his heartbeat reassured her that they were both still alive. Here, with his arm around her, she felt safe. As if together they could beat anything that tried to come after them.

It was over. Marshall and Emma were safe. She was safe. They'd done this together.

She tensed in his embrace. No, they hadn't. She'd tried to do it on her own.

Marshall had come after her.

He'd come *for* her.

As the sound of numerous sirens faded into the distance, a new sound grew inside Rachel. But this one had nothing to do with fear and alarm.

It was safety and security.

It was love.

Unlike Robert, who had shut her out and had run from her at every chance that presented itself, Marshall had run toward her.

He'd put his life in danger for her.

He'd left the safety of his home and the protection of her team to lay down his life for her. He'd had no guarantee that Thalia would figure out where he was in time. No way of knowing what he was walking into back in that cave. No way to defend himself.

But he'd put her life before his. Just like he did for Emma.

The last of the ice thawed around her heart. For the first time since she'd finalized the death of her first marriage, the way was clear for someone else to love her.

For her to love someone else.

As lights scattered through the trees and the sirens grew almost deafening in their intensity, Rachel shoved aside everything that had happened and focused on the man beside her. And while the truth was evident to her and probably to anyone else involved in the situation, she wanted to hear him say it. He'd shown her, but she wanted to hear the words. "Marshall…"

"What?" His voice was a low rumble in his chest, and his heartbeat revved higher, almost as if he knew what she was going to ask him.

"Why did you come tonight?"

Voices sounded near the road, calling to one another as police officers and EMTs drew near. Medical personnel would take her away from him to evaluate her, and she needed to know first.

Rachel pulled away from him and set aside the rest of her fear to ask the question she needed answered more than any other. Sliding from his arms, she grasped his wrists and pinned his gaze. She wanted to see him when he said it and to paint this moment in her mind so that it covered the horrors of Sergeant Wylie Joseph's treachery and turned this night into an entirely different kind of memory. "Why did you come here? You could have stayed home safe with Emma. You could have—"

With a soft smile, he laid his forehead against hers. "You needed me." The words were a breath against her lips, barely audible in the approaching pandemonium, but what her ears strained to grasp, her heart definitely heard. "I promise to always be here when you need me."

His lips hovered dangerously close to hers, but he didn't close the gap. The kiss didn't come.

Disappointment washed over her, threatening to ice over her thawed heart, but then she remembered whom she was dealing with. Captain Marshall Slater was a man of infinite patience. A man who'd wait for her to give before he took.

A man who needed her to reassure him as much as she'd needed him to reassure her.

So she tilted her head to the side and let her lips find his, telling him in a way words never could that she'd given up her fears. They'd find a way to work this out.

She was choosing him.

* * *

Christmas Eve dawned clear, a brand-new three-inch snowfall covering everything in pure white. Em's swing set looked like someone had sprayed whipped cream on all the flat surfaces, and they reflected like glitter in the early-morning sun. It was kind of like a clean start after all the ugly that had taken place over the past week.

Rolling his eyes, Marshall let the blinds drop into place over the kitchen window. He needed more coffee. A glance at the clock on the microwave told him he still had a couple of hours before he could head up to the hospital to see Rachel. The EMTs had whisked her away from him the instant Marshall had told them she'd been drugged. That kiss… that promise she'd made him without saying a word had still been warm on his lips.

And he hadn't seen her since. Yesterday, the doctors had banned visitors from her room, citing the need for rest in the wake of her attack and the exhaustion she was suffering from too long without good sleep.

But this morning? He wasn't missing a minute of the time he could get with her before duty called her back to Camp McGee.

Grabbing his crutches, he walked gingerly

around the kitchen island and punched the button on the coffeepot Wes had prepped the night before.

Wes.

Marshall watched the first drops of coffee drip into the pot.

Emma's grandfather had not been happy when he awoke yesterday morning and found out what Marshall had done overnight. Though he hadn't said a word, his stern expression had spoken volumes about his disapproval. That, and he was likely not very happy he'd been left out of the loop. It had taken him all day to work through his frustration, but he'd seemed fine by dinner.

Footsteps on the stairs in the living room turned Marshall away from the coffeepot.

The front door opened, and a few seconds later, Wes strode into the kitchen wearing pajama pants and a World's Greatest Grandpa sweatshirt. His expression wasn't exactly happy. Guess they were resetting to yesterday's disapproval. "Do you not get a paper?"

"Does anybody get the paper anymore?" Marshall tilted his head to the side. "You don't even get a paper at home, do you?"

"You have no idea what I do at home."

Marshall leaned back against the counter and dragged his hand across his head, trying to scrub some sense into this conversation. Maybe Wes had slept poorly, or he'd dreamed about Maggie. He'd once confessed to Marshall that happened quite frequently. "Coffee will be ready soon. That'll clear your brain fog."

"I don't have any brain fog."

Somebody was grumpy this morning. "Is everything okay, Wes?" Typically Maggie's father was the definition of a morning person. Maybe the stress of the past few days had affected them all.

Wes pulled a chair from the table and sat, resting his forearm on the tabletop. He drummed his fingers on the wood as he eyed his son-in-law with a look that said he was putting the words in his head into some sort of order. Finally, he stopped tapping. "You love Captain Rachel, don't you?"

Marshall chuckled. Apparently, Emma's nickname for Rachel had spread. He grabbed two mugs from the cabinet and settled them on the granite counter. Filling them to the rim, he pivoted and set them on the island.

Wes jumped up and grabbed them, setting the coffee on the table as Marshall retrieved his crutches and hobbled around the island to join him.

Marshall took a bracing sip before he answered Wes's question. "Yes. But I'll always love Maggie. I've never stopped. You made me realize the other night, though, that—"

Holding up his free hand, Wes sliced the thought in two. "I don't doubt that. Maggie loved you the best she could after everything that happened to her. And I'm pretty sure that, next to me, you're the world's greatest dad."

As if on cue, tiny footsteps thundered in the hallway above their heads. Em was up and ready to race into her day.

Glancing at the ceiling, Wes stood and picked up his coffee cup. He passed behind Marshall, clamping a hand on his shoulder. "I just wanted you to know that you deserve to be happy." With a quick squeeze, he walked into the living room, greeting Emma with a boisterous "Good morning, chipmunk."

"Morning, Grampa. Gotta find Daddy." Her footsteps didn't slow until she came into the kitchen and spotted Marshall at the table. She skidded to a halt in her fuzzy socks and stared at him as though she was surprised to see him. Her ever-present pigtails and pink Dora pajamas were the picture of innocence.

Innocence she'd get to keep with Wylie Joseph out of the picture.

Marshall shook off the horrors of the week

and held out his arms to his daughter for a hug. "You want pancakes for breakfast?"

"I have a special delivery." She was so formal and standing so straight with her hands tucked behind her back.

Marshall bit the inside of his lower lip to keep from smiling at what was obviously a serious thing for his little girl. When he felt like he had himself in check, he nodded solemnly. "It's not Christmas morning yet."

"This is a special Christmas Eve present." All the formality fell away, and she raced to him, leaping onto his lap and drawing a wince he hoped she didn't see. She plunked a small box on the table in front of him. About the size of a deck of cards folded in half, it was wrapped in generic green paper with a small red bow on top.

"Did you wrap this?" Marshall picked up the package and inspected it. It was better than he could have done. Then again, he was a notoriously horrible wrapper.

She just giggled and poked the present. "Open it."

Whatever she'd picked out for him at the little Christmas store her school ran for the children, she sure was excited about it. Peeling back the paper slowly to draw out the drama, he made guesses at the contents. "Is it a horse?"

More little-girl laughter washed over his soul, healing some of the anxiety and pain of the past week. "Then the box would have holes in it, Daddy."

"True." He'd let it slide that the box wasn't even big enough to hold a horse's bridle. Popping the small brown box open, he peeked inside. Nestled in brown velvet was a woman's diamond solitaire.

Uh-oh. Someone had mixed up the packages and given Emma the fake ring some disappointed mom wasn't going to get this year. "Um, Em? I think somebody made a mistake."

She leaned forward and looked into the box. "Nope." Her giggles launched again.

Okay, he'd play along. Pulling the ring from the box, he slid it to the first knuckle on his pinkie finger. "It's a little bit small for me."

Her laughter nearly tumbled her out of his lap. "Because it's not for you."

"I'm confused, munchkin." He tightened his grip on her before she bounced onto the floor in her overwrought hysterics. His entire house was off-kilter this morning, in the best of ways.

"It's actually for me."

The voice in the doorway nearly made him leap to his feet until the pain reminded him he couldn't. Marshall reflexively drew his daughter closer as he looked up.

Rachel leaned against the door frame, a sheepish smile on her face and her cheeks a pleasant shade of pink. Wearing jeans and a gray hoodie, her hair up in that ever-present ponytail, she gave him a small wave that was uncharacteristic for her usual confident, take-charge manner.

Marshall couldn't tear his eyes away from her. She looked tired, exactly the way she should after the ordeal she'd been through, but she was definitely stronger than the last time he'd seen her.

When she'd kissed him almost out of his mind.

Never looking away from her, he kissed the back of his daughter's head. "Run and see what your grandpa is doing."

"Okay." Sliding off his lap, she paused only long enough to give Rachel a quick hug around her waist, then trotted into the den.

That had gone easier than he'd expected. It was almost like Em had been coached to deliver the ring and then scatter.

Wait.

The ring.

The ring for Rachel.

His fingers gripped the box tighter and he finally tore his gaze from Rachel to look at it again. It was a single solitaire in a simple gold band. His heart thudded against his rib cage. "You…" His voice crackled and popped, so he swallowed and tried again. "You bought your own Christmas present?"

When he looked up, Rachel was pulling a chair from the table. She turned it and sat, knee to knee with him. "It's from the gift shop at the hospital. I didn't actually have time to go shopping for the real thing. But I did have a lot of time to think yesterday, and…" She reached for the box and wrapped her fingers around his, warm and so right. "And I'm certain I'm in love with you. So I decided that for Christmas I want you to ask me to marry you."

His heart stopped. He was sure of it. Right at the moment he was about to be whole again, it stopped. And when it beat next, it was entirely for her. "You're awfully sure I want to."

She drew her lower lip between her teeth and tipped her head from side to side, smiling. "Well, that kiss you gave me night before last was pretty—"

"I think you kissed me." Not that it mattered. He was about to repeat the performance right now. "And I love you." He leaned toward her, but her hand on his chest stopped him.

"Ask me." Her whisper was almost too quiet to hear, but her eyes said it all anyway.

"What about our jobs?"

She smiled wider. "We'll figure it out together."

"Hmm. I have entertained the thought of becoming an instructor so I can be closer to Emma. Or of becoming a househusband." He grinned and set the box on the table, then pulled out the ring. Holding it up between them, he drew out the moment until he felt like he'd come out of his skin. "So, Captain Rachel. Will—"

"Yes." She closed the space between them and kissed him with even deeper emotion than she had after her rescue. This was more than *I love you*.

This was forever.

* * * * *

Dear Reader,

I hope you enjoyed Marshall and Rachel's Christmas adventure. Writing their story involved a lot of slow moments. A lot of times when it took prayer and really thinking through their lives. They both carried wounds from their pasts. They both believed lies about themselves. They both had to make their way to the truth.

That was one of the reasons I chose John 10:10 as the guiding verse for their story. It's important that we understand that Satan will use everything at his disposal to "steal and kill and destroy." That's not just talking about things. It's talking about the entirety of our lives—relationships, sense of self, callings—and even our eternity. Oh, dear reader, how I pray that you have replaced Satan's lies with God's truth, that you know with certainty who God created you to be and how very much He loves you!

If you'd like to say hello, I'd love for you to drop by www.jodiebailey.com to see what's new or to drop me a note. As always, I'm praying for you!

Jodie Bailey

Get 4 FREE REWARDS!

We'll send you 2 FREE Books plus 2 FREE Mystery Gifts.

Love Inspired Suspense books showcase how courage and optimism unite in stories of faith and love in the face of danger.

FREE Value Over **$20**

HARLEQUIN SELECTS COLLECTION

19 FREE BOOKS IN ALL!

From Robyn Carr to RaeAnne Thayne to Linda Lael Miller and Sherryl Woods we promise (actually, GUARANTEE!) each author in the Harlequin Selects collection has seen their name on the *New York Times* or *USA TODAY* bestseller lists!

Visit
ReaderService.com
Today!

As a valued member of the Harlequin Reader Service, you'll find these benefits and more at ReaderService.com:

- Try 2 free books from any series
- Access risk-free special offers
- View your account history & manage payments
- Browse the latest Bonus Bucks catalog

Don't miss out!

If you want to stay up-to-date on the latest at the Harlequin Reader Service and enjoy more content, make sure you've signed up for our monthly News & Notes email newsletter. Sign up online at ReaderService.com or by calling Customer Service at 1-800-873-8635.